Operation Timewarp

Kate Reid

Dolphin Paperbacks

First published in Great Britain in 2002
by Dolphin Paperbacks,
a division of the Orion Publishing Group Ltd
Orion House
5 Upper St Martin's Lane
London WC2H 9EA

A catalogue record for this book
is available from the British Library

ISBN 1 84255 203 1

Typeset at The Spartan Press Ltd,
Lymington, Hants

Printed and bound in Great Britain by
Clays Ltd, St Ives plc

For Stephen and Frank Polatch

Contents

part one
Recruitment

1
Rounded Up

When I look back on it all, I'm glad I smashed that glass. If I hadn't, we might have stayed on the PlayStation all day. Then they might have picked some other people, and trained them up to use the stun guns instead of us. And we would never have seen the future at all.

We first met them one afternoon in the last week of the summer holidays. I was on the PlayStation with my brother Elliot and we had the curtains tightly drawn – partly to keep the brightness off the screen, and partly because Elliot had this mad idea that a huge dog was staring in at him through the French windows.

Elliot was pretty good on the PlayStation, for someone his age, but in a game like the one we were playing, where you have to fight alongside each other, he had a tendency to fall off cliffs and get killed, so he couldn't back me up properly. That was what happened that morning and in the end I gave up in disgust. I picked up this furry pig we won at the fair.

'You're rubbish, Elliot,' I said. 'I'd be better off playing with him.'

'Yeah, right,' he said. 'You and the pig would make a great team. You look the same and you smell the same.'

So I lobbed the pig at him and his glass got smashed and a load of milk went everywhere.

Our mum stuck her head round the door.

'I can't believe you're fighting again. And why are you sitting in the dark? Get out and get some fresh air. Clear out your shed or something, like you said you would.'

'Oh, Mum,' said Elliot. 'It's still two weeks to the car boot sale. We don't have to do the shed today.'

She ignored him.

'Take these with you, Adam,' she said, holding out a new roll of black bin bags. 'Then you can sort the stuff in the shed into rubbish and car boot. But make sure you get back here by six. We're going bowling with the Owens, remember.'

I'm good at bowling and I would normally have enjoyed it. Except that by six o'clock, they'd recruited Elliot and me and a girl we hardly knew for a secret and dangerous mission – which kind of took my mind off the balls.

To get to our shed, you climb over the wall at the end of our garden, cross the road, crawl under the barbed wire fence into the wasteland and pick your way through a load of brambles, stingers and broken glass. Then you just have to battle with our rusty old padlock and you're in.

The police sealed it off later, of course, but we didn't mind. It's not really our shed. We just took it over a few years ago, because nobody else used it. There was only one other boy in the road then, and in those days we hated him and he hated us.

4

I hated Lewis because he broke my bike and because whenever he saw Elliot or me he'd shout: 'Freak Alert! Freak Alert!' and make a weird siren noise.

Also, Lewis never let me borrow his skateboard, even though he never used it himself. And once, when we were wrestling, Lewis joined in on my side and bent Elliot's arm right up behind his back. It really hurt Elliot and I didn't want anything to do with Lewis after that.

We hadn't seen much of him that summer, anyway, because he had someone new to pick on. A girl called Tara and her mum had just moved in with him and his dad, and when we clambered over our wall, there she was in the road, rollerblading.

'Hi Tara! Nice blades,' said Elliot.

Elliot was only eight that summer, and he was really friendly to everyone still, even girls and people he didn't know.

'Hi Elliot!' said Tara, giving him a lovely smile. 'How's things?'

But he wasn't even looking at her any more. He was staring down the road towards the garages with a look of terror on his face.

'There it is, Adam,' he said, clutching my arm. 'Like I told you. Horrible fangs and green eyes!'

Sniffing around down by the garages was an enormous Alsatian dog, which turned, head low, eyes glinting, and stared right at us.

Suddenly Elliot pegged it to the gap under the barbed wire fence. The dog came loping towards us and I caught Elliot's fear and so did Tara and we legged it after him. I got under quickly, right after Elliot, but Tara got stuck, because of her rollerblades. I held up the wire of the fence for her and, as the dog got closer, I saw it really did have green eyes. They were unnaturally bright green, almost fluorescent.

I reached up and lobbed the roll of bin bags hard at the dog's head. The dog bared its sharp yellow teeth at me and threw back its head and barked like a madman. At last, Tara got under the wire and we stumbled through the wet brambles to where Elliot was struggling with the rusty old lock. We could hear the dog behind us scrabbling under the fence and panting through the trees.

Then Elliot shouted 'Yes!' and we pushed into the shed, slamming the door and shoving back the heavy bolt we'd fixed on the inside. We were all panting and trembling, leaning our heads against the door and getting our breath back, when a loud cough from the back of the shed made us jump.

'We meet at last,' said a voice. 'My name is Steiner.'

We peered through the gloom and saw – sitting on the rotting chest of drawers, amongst the piles of junk – a very old man. Even in the dim light, I could see that his eyes were the same fluorescent green as the dog's.

2
Mission Briefing

'I'm so pleased you could come,' said Steiner, standing up stiffly. 'And I'm delighted to meet you at last, because we have a mission for you, should you choose to accept it.'

To which none of us said anything at all. We just stared at him. Steiner was pretty cool-looking for an old man. He had a bald head, a white moustache and bushy eyebrows and he was dressed in an immaculate grey suit, with a jacket like a cape.

'Perhaps you would like to meet the others before you decide?' he said.

We watched in horror as he rolled up the old red rug to reveal a brand new trapdoor set in the wooden floor of the shed.

We all looked at each other and, quick as a flash, Tara shot back the bolt and pushed open the shed door again ready to run for it. There was a frenzy of barking and she slammed it shut again, but we could still hear snarling and scrabbling outside.

'Who let the dogs out, or what?' said Elliot under his breath.

'Please stay, my dear,' said Steiner to Tara. 'We haven't come to harm you, but to ask for your help in our time of need.'

'Call off that horrible dog then,' said Tara. 'Please.'

I nodded furiously.

The old man took a small gadget out of his pocket and spoke into it.

'Return to base,' he said, and the snarling and scrabbling stopped.

'He's a nutter,' breathed Tara, into my ear. 'We've got to run for it.'

She opened the door again and clattered off on her rollerblades. I beckoned to Elliot, then raced after her. We got as far as the barbed wire fence before we realised that Elliot wasn't with us.

'I'll have to go back and get him,' I said, with a sinking feeling.

'I'll come with you,' said Tara, for which I was very grateful.

We couldn't believe what we saw inside; Elliot was actually helping the old man with the trapdoor.

'It's all right,' said Elliot cheerfully. 'He's come from the future and he needs our help. He's not a weirdo or anything.'

'Indeed I'm not,' said Steiner, looking a bit shocked. 'So do come back in.'

I looked at Tara and she nodded. As we went back in, the trapdoor was flung right open and a woman climbed out. She was in silver combat gear, with a holster on her hip, and she too had those bright green eyes.

'Aren't you lovely!' she said, looking at us. 'Even more gorgeous than my real niece and nephews . . . and so brave.' She came over and shook our hands warmly.

She was very pretty, but clearly just as crazy as the old man. She turned back to Steiner and started scolding him.

'Poor darlings,' she said. 'Their hands are shaking. How many times did I tell you not to use Wilson's beastly old dog?'

'Approximately thirty-eight times,' said Steiner. 'But you must admit that Rex did round them up most effectively. Perhaps you could stop criticising me and help me explain it all.'

'OK, OK,' she said, 'Keep your hair on.'

'Too late for that,' said Elliot under his breath.

The woman turned to look at us, thoughtfully.

'Take a seat, my dears,' she said.

We sat down on the old beanbags, but I felt extremely anxious.

'My name is Liz McCoy,' she began.

'Hello,' said my brother.

'Hello Elliot,' said Liz, and I wondered how she knew his name. 'We have come to you from the year 2099 . . .'

'From the loonybin, more like,' said Tara quietly.

'From the year 2099,' said Liz firmly. 'It may seem strange, lovey, but it's quite true. Take a look.'

She took something out of her pocket. 'Play Town Scene,' she said and a 3D image appeared, transforming the old shed into an IMAX cinema. It showed our town, but not as we knew it. We saw a sort of flying car hovering and landing on the top of the police headquarters and a group of young people on skateboard things flying along past the law courts and the statue of the horse.

'2099,' said Liz, switching off the projector. 'What do you think?'

'I like that hovering car,' said Elliot, zooming a flat hand noisily through the air and landing it neatly on my shoulder.

Tara looked at me with wide eyes.

'She's for real,' she said. 'They are from the year 2099.'

I nodded in agreement and as I did so my anxiety changed to excitement. There was something about that 3D scene that was totally convincing. You see, it wasn't glamorous and exciting like a movie, it was real and everyday like the news.

'OK,' said Tara, calmly. 'So you really are from the year 2099. But what do you want with us?'

'We're in a spot of trouble, flower,' said Liz. 'We need some outside help . . . from some people with the right stuff . . . and we've picked on you three.'

'We're the chosen ones,' said Elliot.

I couldn't sit still any longer. 'What have we been chosen for?' I shouted and jumped to my feet.

'It's a bit cramped in the shed, Steiner,' said Liz. 'Why don't we go down to the garage? We could show them the time machine and tell them all about it.'

We looked at each other and nodded. I found myself following the others through the trapdoor and down a very tall ladder. I don't like heights much, so I was glad when my feet touched ground. There was a door down there. Liz knocked on it and another old man stuck his head round.

'Meet Wilson,' said Steiner. 'My right-hand man and trusted factotum.'

Wilson smiled at us modestly. I couldn't see whether he had those green eyes, because they were hidden behind tinted glasses. He was dressed like Steiner but he was shorter and stouter and something about his tinted glasses suddenly gave me the creeps. I decided it was madness to go underground with a load of old weirdos. I was about to grab Elliot and run, when Wilson flung open the door to the garage.

Inside I saw inflatable beds and a sofa, some kind of metal vending machine and, floating in the air, a bright red hovercar! It was older and more battered than the one on the film, but it still blew me away.

'Come on board,' said Liz.

I was excited as we followed her up the rusty steps and through the hatch. There were five cracked leather seats inside and loads of cool controls, like a fighter jet. There was no roof or separate doors and windows, just one large bubble of rather dirty glass.

'Prepare for lightspeed, Chewie,' said Elliot, sitting down in the driver's seat.

'As you see,' said Liz, ignoring him, 'the time machine is just like any regular hovercar, except for this.'

She showed us an insignificant little switch.

'It's a deadly secret.'

We looked more closely and Liz showed us tiny letters scratched at each end of the switch – the letters S and T.

'Can anybody guess what the letters stand for?' asked Liz.

'Something and time?' I said.

'Sausages and tomato ketchup?' said Elliot.

'Space and time,' said Tara.

'Quite right,' said Liz. 'In space mode you travel from place to place. In time mode you stay put, but travel to another time. It's simpler really, as there's no steering involved. You simply set the switch to T, then select the date and time here. Then you use this red button to send out the probe and press *Go* when you're ready. Can anybody guess why Finn included a probe in his design?'

'To stop you landing smack on top of someone and squashing 'em to a squish?' said Elliot, inspired.

'That's right,' said Liz, ruffling Elliot's hair.

'Who's Finn?' asked Tara.

'Finn is the friend, comrade and genius who invented time travel,' said Steiner, sticking his bald head up through the hatch. 'He made this whole operation possible.'

'What operation?' I asked.

'Operation Timewarp,' said Steiner grandly.

'Come and have something to eat,' said Liz, 'and we'll tell you all about it.'

Liz took us down to the vending machine in the corner of the garage.

'It's a food replicator,' said Liz. 'Step up close and tell it what you want to eat.'

Elliot stood there thinking for a ridiculously long time, then he asked for sausage and chips and a bottle of coke. The machine hummed. A green light came on and a flap opened to reveal a tray with a plate of food, a knife and fork, a bottle and a straw. I asked the machine for chicken and chips and Sprite, and Tara had Thai green curry and pineapple juice. We sat down on the inflatable sofa to eat. It was all great and the chips were those lovely thin ones.

Steiner asked the machine for a bourbon biscuit and a semi-skimmed, decaff cappuccino, dusted lightly with plain chocolate. Then he sat on the steps of the hovercar.

'Get the projector, would you, Wilson,' he said. 'I think we left it up in the shed.'

Wilson muttered something but went off obediently to get it.

'Brave young people,' said Steiner, taking a sip of froth. 'We have come to ask for your help in overthrowing a cruel tyrant.'

Why can't they do it themselves? I thought.

'We cannot do it ourselves,' said Steiner, fixing me with his intense green gaze. 'We need the help of some spirited young people, and in our time there are none.'

'Why not?' said Tara.

'It's a sorry business,' Steiner sighed. 'You know what genes are, I trust?'

'I do,' said Elliot, stabbing one of his sausages with a fork. 'They decide whether you've got blue eyes or brown and whether you have normal ears like me or sticking-out ones like Adam.'

Tara snorted, but Steiner took no notice.

'Your scientists recently mapped the entire human genetic code,' he said, dunking his biscuit in his coffee. 'It was a great triumph, because we were able to eradicate a number of terrible diseases. It was also a great disaster, because parents were able to select the kind of children they preferred.

'There was a lot of foolish talk in those days about young people being out of control. So parents chose not to have children with genes thought to cause troublesome behaviour such as alcohol and drug addiction, criminality and aggression. Soon there was peace and quiet at home and at school. The few unruly children that were left were given medication to calm them down. Soon there were no unruly children at all. Our young people never fight, tell lies, break rules or disobey their elders . . .'

'But they've got no spirit,' interrupted Wilson, who'd come back with the projector.

'No Indomitable Spirit,' said Elliot.

Everyone looked puzzled.

'It's one of the five tenets of this martial art, Tae Kwon-Do,' I explained. 'We had to learn them – indomitable spirit, courtesy, self-control and two others.'

'We had to give it up,' said Elliot, through a mouthful of chips. 'But we sometimes do Ju-Jitsu instead.'

'Courtesy and self-control?' murmured Steiner. 'Was that all that was needed? After all, human nature is the result of centuries of evolution. Why did we ever presume to better it?'

'At least you got rid of people like my stepbrother Lewis,' said Tara, putting her empty plate down on the floor.

'It takes all sorts to make a world,' said Steiner. 'And that includes Lewis . . .'

Tara looked doubtful, but Steiner rambled on.

I stopped listening. I ate my chicken and watched Elliot. He had finished his meal and he was busy counting something in the palm of his hand – his bangers, twists of white paper that explode when you throw them at the ground. They were Elliot's most treasured possessions and he counted them carefully, then stuffed them back in his pocket.

At last, Tara interrupted.

'Excuse me, Mr Steiner,' she said. 'You haven't said what you want us to do.'

'Apologies,' said Steiner. 'We are ruled by a tyrant and we need your help to get rid of him. Show them, Elizabeth!' he said.

'Play President Rigg and the clones,' said Liz, taking the projector from Wilson.

A 3D image appeared on the rusty steps of the hovercar. We saw a burly middle-aged man with a heavy face, pale blue eyes and a thick black moustache. He was wearing camouflage gear and a black beret and he smiled heartily as a group of younger men arrived. The young men were all heavily armed and all equally tall and thickset. They all had blue eyes and black hair like the president, but some had moustaches, some were cleanshaven, some had shaved their hair and others had it long in a ponytail. Apart from that they were identical. A door opened and a frail-looking elderly man was shoved through. They started to push him around. He fell over, but they made him get up again. When he couldn't get up any more, some of them started to kick him. I felt sick and I was glad when Liz switched off.

'President Rigg and some of his charming clones,' said Steiner. 'Cloning's illegal of course, but that didn't stop Rigg. He's got an army of one thousand eighteen-year-old thugs – all genetically identical to himself.'

'They do whatever they like,' said Wilson grimly, looking at me through his tinted glasses. 'If you get in their way, you get hurt, like the gentleman in the film.'

'Come on Elliot,' I said, standing up. 'We're out of here. We can't take on armed men. Let's face it, we've been known to run away from Lewis's super-soaker.'

'Wait, Adam,' said Liz gently, 'sit down and let me explain.'

She showed us a 3D image of Buckingham Palace in London.

'Rigg's HQ,' she said. 'It's heavily guarded and adults can't get near it, but Rigg has no reason to fear young people like yourselves. They're all far too docile to cause him any trouble. Rigg has a daughter, Stella. Your first objective will be to make friends with Stella and get an invitation to the Palace. Further objectives will be to locate an access point to the security system, then shut it down. Steiner's team will take it from there.

'You will live with me,' Liz continued, smiling warmly. 'My sister, Amy McCoy, has three children. They've gone into hiding so that you can impersonate them.'

'I got Wilson here to spread rumours that Amy McCoy won the lottery and went away to have cosmetic surgery,' said Steiner. 'Meanwhile, her children – you three – have moved to London to stay with their aunt and attend Stella Rigg's excellent school.'

'But why can't the real McCoys do it?' asked Elliot.

'Because they can't tell lies and break rules,' said Tara.

'Not even for a good reason?'

'No, lovey,' said Liz. 'Our young people would be too scared.'

'What makes you think we won't be?' said Elliot. 'I get scared occasionally.'

'I got Wilson to put a camera on that dog,' said Steiner. 'We've been admiring your behaviour. Of course you get scared sometimes, but when you're angry or you need to help someone, you can overcome it.'

'But why us three?' asked Tara. 'We're nothing special.'

'Maybe not,' said Wilson dryly. 'But you were the right ages and you were just round the corner, so Steiner thought you'd do.'

Nobody spoke for a while as Liz showed us how to feed our bottles, plates and cutlery back into the food replicator.

'Will you help us?' she said.

'I'd like to ask the audience,' said Elliot, looking at me.

'We'll have to ask our parents,' I said.

'No need,' said Liz. 'You can return to the very same time at which you leave. They won't even know you've been away.'

I didn't know what to say.

'No pressure,' said Steiner. 'But you are our only hope.'

'I'm up for it,' said Tara. 'I need a break from Lewis and his dad, anyway.'

I wanted to go too. I didn't like seeing that old man kicked around and I really wanted to help. I also wanted to try the hoverboards and cars and everything else in the future – but if I'd known then how dangerous it would be, there's no way I would ever have agreed to go.

'Are you sure we'll be safe?' I asked.

'Totally,' said Steiner. 'We're giving you state-of-the-art defensive weapons.'

That clinched it for me. 'OK then,' I said.

'Cool!' said Elliot, punching the air.

'Marvellous,' said Liz.

'We are very grateful,' said Steiner.

'Very grateful indeed,' said Wilson.

'Can I see the defensive weapons?' said Elliot.

'The stun guns?' said Liz. 'Of course, we can show you how to use them now.'

'Yikes,' I said, looking at my watch. 'It's nearly six. We've got to get home.'

'We've got to go bowling,' explained Elliot. 'If we don't turn up, Mum will come looking for us. Why don't you come too, Tara? Mum won't mind.'

'Thanks,' said Tara, looking pleased.

'You all want to go bowling?' said Wilson in disbelief. Then he turned to Steiner. 'They're mere kids, Steiner. I really think you should reconsider the whole operation.'

'Leave the decision-making to me please, Wilson,' said Steiner. 'If Sir Francis Drake could take time out for a bit of bowling, why shouldn't these three do the same?'

Wilson shrugged. Like me, he probably didn't know what Steiner was on about.

We said goodbye and agreed to come back for training in the morning.

I was first up the long metal ladder. I wasn't enjoying it,

but I was nearly at the top – when a rung suddenly came off in my hand.

There was a sickening lurch as I grabbed on wildly with my other hand but that rung came away too and I swung backwards into the void.

3
Armed and Dangerous

I was dangling upside down with my head banging painfully against the metal. I would have fallen, except that my feet had hooked on and Tara stopped my fall.

'You nearly knocked me off,' said Tara shakily. 'What are you playing at?'

'Bats?' I said.

Clutching on grimly to the edges of the ladder, I slowly managed to right myself. The two missing rungs had been sawn through at each end. So had the next four. They were held in place with chewing gum, but they came away easily when I touched them, falling to the ground with a sickening clang.

'We'd better get down,' I said. 'The ladder's not safe.'

We climbed down to the bottom, where Steiner and Liz were examining the fallen rungs.

'Who could have done such a terrible thing?' said Steiner.

'My stepbrother Lewis,' said Tara. 'He's always spying on me. He probably followed us here.'

'Yep,' said Elliot. 'And he hates us. We bolted the shed door, but he must have broken in.'

I was shocked about the ladder. I can be pretty annoying, in class and stuff, but as far as I was aware, nobody had ever tried to kill me before.

'Don't take it personally,' said Tara. 'Lewis couldn't know that you'd go up first.'

I wasn't so sure.

We sneaked out through the garage door into Greenhill Road and walked home up the hill. Elliot won the bowling, because the day's events had totally shaken me up.

The next morning, we met Tara by the shed, ready for our stun gun training. We found a note inside, taped to the trapdoor.

Ladder fixed. Come on down.

In the garage, Steiner was supervising Wilson, who was inflating a big pile of mattresses by throwing them into the air.

'The noble volunteers,' he cried as we opened the door. 'Good morning to you.'

'You fixed the ladder then, Mr Steiner,' said Elliot.

'Yes, yes,' he said. 'Curious incident. No sign of a break-in and the shed door was still bolted on the inside until we opened it for you this morning.'

'Maybe Lewis slipped the bolt from the outside using wire,' said Elliot. 'Like a car thief.'

'Maybe,' said Steiner, vaguely. 'There was a lot of crime in your day, a lot of it drug related. I expect you three sometimes indulge in a spot of shoplifting, don't you?'

'We do not,' I said indignantly.

But Steiner had turned back to Wilson.

'Cover the whole floor with those mattresses, Wilson, there's a good chap.'

Liz emerged from the hovercar.

'Good morning flowers,' she said. 'Are you ready for your target practice?'

She came down and sprayed a lifesize outline of a man on the wall. He had a big black moustache, so you could tell it was meant to be President Rigg.

I've never wanted to blow anyone's head off or anything, but I had a go with an air rifle once and I really enjoyed it. So I was excited when Liz handed us our weapons.

'Finn made them using ordinary mobile phone cases,' she said. 'You can use them as phones, but don't let anyone else borrow them. They're top secret.'

I'd never had my own mobile before, let alone a customised stun gun one. I looked at it eagerly. Each one came with a holster and had a concealed button on the back. When you pressed it, a trigger handle clicked out. When you squeezed the trigger, it fired a dart containing a powerful anaesthetic. That morning, we practised with blanks.

The first one up was Elliot. Liz told him to take aim and fire. Of course, Elliot really went for it. He whipped the mobile out of his holster, clicked out the trigger handle, flung his arm right out and fired. Bam! The dart buried itself in the wall, a metre wide of Rigg's head, and Elliot went flying backwards and landed flat on his back.

'Yowch!'

'Now you know why we put the mats out,' said Liz.

Then Tara took careful aim, braced herself and fired. Bam! The dart struck the wall just above Rigg's head and she staggered backwards and fell on top of Elliot.

They were still laughing like madmen when I took my turn. I clicked out the trigger handle, aimed and fired. I tottered but I didn't fall. I had hit Rigg in the chest.

'Great shot,' said Liz. 'You're a natural.

'We're going to practise until it's second nature,' she went on. 'You'll probably never need to use these things, but if things get nasty, you cannot afford to miss.'

By the end of the morning, I could hit Rigg from anywhere, without fail. I even tried it from the hovercar hatch and got him right in the forehead.

You could tell Liz was dead pleased.

'Cease fire!' she shouted. 'It's time for a well-deserved lunch.'

Liz asked the food replicator for four burgers, four glasses of fruit juice cocktail and a family bowl of lightning chips. The burgers tasted as if they'd been barbecued in a lemon and lime sauce. The lightning chips were delicious and they set off little sparks in your mouth. The drink was red and fizzy and floating with strawberries and cherries.

'Down with Rigg!' said Liz, raising her glass – and we all drank to that.

'By the way,' said Tara. 'What happened to the Queen?'

'What queen?' said Liz.

'I mean if Rigg is in Buckingham Palace, what happened to the royals?'

'I'm a bit hazy on history, sweetheart. I think there

might have been a scandal and a resignation or something. We just have a president now.'

'So who's going to be president when you get rid of Rigg?' I asked.

'We'll have elections, I suppose,' said Liz, picking a cherry out of her drink and nibbling it. 'You'd better ask Steiner. He's a government type.'

'Is he a politician?' said Tara.

'He used to be Mayor of London until Rigg forced him out. Wilson ran for mayor too, but it was Steiner who won the election. They used to be great rivals in those days, but Wilson is Steiner's right-hand man now . . . along with Finn.'

'So Finn's his left-hand man?' said Elliot.

'In a way, but he's an outlaw and he has to live in hiding. He's a genius, you see, and Rigg would love to get his hands on his extraordinary brainpower.'

'What's Finn like?'

'He is special; he's a GMO.'

'A Genetically Modified Organism?' said Tara.

Liz nodded.

'Like a tomato?' said Elliot. 'Cool.'

'There were only two made like him. He's supposed to be the result of an illegal experiment in Scotland. His genes aren't all human, there's something else in the mix.'

'Are there loads of weird GM things?' said Elliot.

'Years ago there was a craze for pigs with wings, that kind of thing. But GM novelties are banned now.'

Lix disappeared into the hovercar, opened up the glass bubble and threw a bag down to Tara.

'Clothes for the journey,' she said, climbing down to join us. 'You'll get more in London.'

There was one set for each of us. I liked mine, especially the shirt, which was made of thin silver material, like soft tinfoil.

Elliot tried all his stuff on. Tara just held her bronze shirt up and looked at herself in the steel side of the food replicator. She saw Liz's face reflected there also.

'I hope you don't mind me asking,' said Tara, 'but why have you all got those amazing green eyes?'

'I'm not sure,' said Liz. 'Maybe too many parents chose the bright green eyes and the gene was so strong it took over. We haven't all got them, but it's rare to see gorgeous brown eyes like yours, Tara. It might look odd in fact, that none of you three have green eyes, but what can we do?'

'We'll get fashion lenses,' said Tara excitedly. 'I know where they sell them.'

She did too, and they cost us a fortune.

'I wish I could come shopping with you guys,' said Liz. 'I'd love to look at all those period costumes.'

'Why don't you?' said Tara.

'Too risky, petal. But could you get something for Finn? It's called Irn-Bru. It was his favourite when he was a kid, but nobody's got the recipe to feed into the reppy.'

Tara took a pad of yellow Post-it notes and a pencil out of her mini backpack and wrote a list:

1. Irn-Bru x 2
2. Contacts — brightest green poss

Then, as an afterthought, she added:

3. Lipgloss. Kiwi?

We said goodbye to Liz and headed for the shops. We arranged to come back the following morning to set off for the year 2099.

We got two cans of Irn-Bru from Pickards and then we went into town to get the bright green contact lenses. They were really expensive and we had to get two pairs each, just in case. The worst thing was that we had to use our own savings, because Steiner didn't have any real money at all. Poor Elliot. He'd been saving up for a skateboard for ages. He wanted to get a really good one with decent wheels and trucks and he had to spend all that money on contact lenses. He began to have mixed feelings about the mission.

That evening, he wrote a note:

Deer Mum (and Dad)
    We have gone to the futyer (yeer 200099) with two old men and Liz to help them get rid of the presedent if you are reeding this we mite be stuck there we will try to get back soon love form adam and Elliot

'They'll just think you're joking,' I said when I'd read the letter through.

'I'll put something in with it then,' said Elliot. 'To convince them.'

'Like what?'

'I dunno . . . one of these socks maybe?'

He stretched out his feet. He'd forgotten to change out of the soft tinfoil socks he'd tried on that morning. He took one off and had a quick sniff.

'Still clean,' he said.

'Wow,' I said. 'That silver material must have cosmic stink-busting properties.'

'Yep,' said Elliot. 'That's why they chose it for your shirt.'

And he put the sock in the envelope with the letter and added a note.

ps sock form 200099

'They'll get it analysed in a lab,' he said. 'And that'll prove it, because you can't get that material yet, can you?'

We left in the morning. Mum had an early shift, so she'd left for the hospital before we got up and we couldn't even say goodbye. I felt uneasy about it, but if what Steiner said was true, it didn't matter how long we stayed in the future. We'd be home again by the time she got back from work.

When we got to the shed, Tara stepped out from behind a bush, grinning.

'Had to hide, in case Lewis followed me here,' she said. 'You do not know how much I need this break from him.'

We went in the shed and bolted up.

We were just about to lift the trapdoor when the door of the shed splintered open and a bulky body crashed through onto the floor.

4
The Gatecrasher

'Gotcha!' said Lewis, triumphantly, standing up and dusting off the splinters. 'I knew you three met up in here.'

Before we had time to say anything, the trapdoor was flung open and Steiner's face appeared. He looked thoroughly taken aback.

'Mr Lewis I presume?' he said at last. He must have recognised him from the dog camera.

Lewis didn't reply and I was pleased to see that he looked absolutely terrified. You couldn't blame him, because Steiner was not looking his best. He had cut himself shaving, there was cappuccino froth in his moustache and his weird green eyes darted manically from Lewis to the splintered door.

'We've got a visitor, Elizabeth,' he said, as he climbed up into the shed. 'What now?'

'Maybe he could come with us, Steiner,' said Liz, clambering out after him. 'If we leave him here, he'll alert other people and that could be a problem.'

'We could hit him with a stun gun dart,' Elliot suggested eagerly.

'Certainly not!' said Steiner.

'How about gagging him, tying him up and leaving him in the shed?' said Elliot. 'Like you said, we'll be back in no time, so he'll be all right.'

'No, no!' said Liz. 'He'd better come with us, Steiner.'

'Welcome on board, Lewis,' said Steiner politely. 'Come on down and we'll show you what's what.'

Lewis made a dash for the door, but Elliot stuck his foot out and tripped him up.

Lewis sprang up and lunged at Elliot. I stepped between them and caught Lewis's fist right in my stomach.

'It's OK, Lewis,' said Elliot. 'Wait till you see their time machine.'

'Time machine?' echoed Lewis and you could tell from his face that he was hooked.

But I was gutted. While the others headed off down the ladder, I straightened up painfully, and grabbed Tara and Steiner's arms.

'We can't take Lewis,' I said. 'He'll ruin everything. We all hate him. He's a bully.'

Steiner's bushy eyebrows shot up in disbelief.

'Adam's right,' said Tara. 'They used to make him take those pills when he was at primary school, the ones that calm you down.'

'He's evil,' I said in agreement and it sounded bonkers even to me.

'Ridiculous,' said Steiner. 'Very few people are evil. I'd say he's been hurt and he's lonely. He feels left out.'

'Left out?' I hissed. 'That's his fault. He never even lets me use his skateboard.'

Steiner looked annoyed.

'Keep your voice down, Adam. We are taking Lewis with us and that's that. I am not asking you to be his best friend, I am just asking you to work with him. I'll ask Finn about him. Finn can see things we can't. Let him judge if Lewis is to be trusted.'

With that, Steiner started to climb down the ladder. Lewis was coming with us and I would just have to lump it.

I decided I'd better warn Elliot to be nice to Lewis, but when I caught up with the others, Elliot was already sitting next to him on the sofa. He was even sharing a bowl of lightning chips with him! I sat down too and as I did so, Lewis turned round to say something to Elliot, knocking the chips and ketchup into my lap.

Perfect, I thought, as I scraped the ketchup off my trousers with a knife. First you break my bike, then you try to kill me, then you gatecrash my adventure, then you spill ketchup in my lap. What are you going to do next?

Liz smiled warmly at Lewis and gave him a set of clothes to try on, but at least Tara wasn't so easily swayed. At one point, she stood up and asked Elliot and me if we wanted a drink from the replicator – cutting Lewis out completely.

I cornered Elliot.

'What about the ladder? Don't you still think it was Lewis that sabotaged it?'

'Nope,' said Elliot. 'You saw how shocked he was when the trapdoor opened. He didn't even know the ladder was there. And if he knew how to unbolt the door, he wouldn't have smashed it down, would he?'

Steiner was drinking one last cup of coffee, supervising Wilson, who was struggling to fold up the deflated beds and sofa. I took him to one side.

'Please Steiner,' I began. 'If it wasn't Lewis who sabotaged the ladder, it must have been one of your team.'

This time Steiner looked really angry. 'My team is one hundred percent loyal,' he said. 'We've decided that the damage was probably inflicted by football hooligans or vandals . . . there was a lot of that in your day.'

Football hooligans? The man was mad. But if Steiner wasn't worried, why should I be? I rejoined the others and changed into my future clothes.

Wilson had stowed all their stuff away in the hovercar, so we had nowhere to sit but the cold garage floor. Steiner called for silence:

'The hour is upon us,' he said. 'We have unexpected company in Lewis here. So please will you all welcome him on board.'

Steiner paused while we all clapped politely. Only Tara's hands were still.

'Lewis will work with Finn at his secret hideout, and I am sure he will provide invaluable assistance to the mission. The three McCoys will be based in London, with Elizabeth, but we will arrange for the four of you to meet up in a few days.'

'Can't wait,' muttered Tara, but Steiner silenced her with a look.

'I am asking you to put aside your old grievances and to work together as friends. We have a chance to make a real difference to the world. Let's take it.'

And he strode off towards the hovercar with a theatrical flourish of his cape.

Liz set the timer to fast-forward us to 04:00 hours on Saturday, 5 September 2099. We would arrive in the early hours of the morning, two days before the start of the school term.

She sent out the probe and I saw the outline of the hovercar amongst the trunks of tall trees.

'All clear,' she said.

Then Steiner addressed us again.

'When we arrive you must all follow Elizabeth swiftly and in ABSOLUTE SILENCE until we get to Finn's. Wilson, you will garage the hovercar, then make your way back to Finn's as soon as you can. Good luck, everyone. Are we ready, Elizabeth?'

'Yes sir!'

It was like a ride I went on once at Alton Towers. My head felt like it was going to explode. When it was over, I peered eagerly through the glass bubble, but all I could see of the future was darkness.

part two

Undercover Operations

5
Finn's Treehouse

We jumped out onto soft springy ground and followed Liz through dense woodland. The fir trees on Greenhill Road, I thought. There seemed to be a park here now, with no sign of any garages or houses. Liz stopped, opened a hidden door in the bark of an enormous tree trunk and disappeared inside. Lewis, Tara and Elliot did the same and I followed after them with Steiner.

'Onwards and upwards now, Adam,' said Steiner.

I hesitated. There was another flipping ladder in front of me, rising straight up inside the tree trunk. Elliot was just starting the long climb.

'Is this operation sponsored by the Acme Ladders Corporation or something?' he said.

We came up into a kind of log cabin, hidden high in the branches of the enormous tree. You could tell it was high, because the floor moved below you like a boat on the sea as the tree swayed in the wind.

There was a bed in one corner and a table laden with books, papers, electronic equipment, mugs and a funny-looking kettle. The wooden floor was strewn with leaves –

and that was where we sat. The cabin was lit by candles, which gave out just enough light to see by, but not enough to be noticed from the ground. The candles lit up the faces of Liz McCoy, the old man Steiner, my brother Elliot, Tara and her stepbrother Lewis. They also lit up the face of Finn, the inventor of time travel, who was smiling at us gently.

Steiner whispered something to Finn, who nodded vigorously.

'Lewis, Adam, Tara, Elliot . . . we are very grateful to you all for coming to our aid,' he said, standing up and shaking us all eagerly by the hand. He was a big, energetic bloke and he looked about forty. He had a Scottish accent and a friendly way of talking and he always had a smile on his face. His skin was a funny grey colour, but that was the only really strange thing about him.

'What did you think of the time machine?' he said. 'Did you have a good trip?'

'It was fine,' said Tara.

'Apart from nearly blowing our heads off,' said Elliot.

'Ah yes . . . I fear there's nothing I can do about that,' he said regretfully. 'But what about the stun guns? I had a bit of trouble with the trigger mechanism. Have you had any problems?'

We shook our heads.

'They're brilliant,' I said.

He beamed.

'The phone function should still work fine too, though my prototype sometimes cuts you off mid-chat. Maybe I'll take another look at them . . .'

'I'm sure they'll work marvellously,' said Steiner, giving Finn a nudge and whispering in his ear again.

'OK, OK,' said Finn and he walked over to Lewis and laid his hands on his head.

'You will be a great asset to the operation, Lewis,' he said solemnly. 'You have a troubled mind, but a good heart.'

Lewis looked up at Finn and his usually grumpy face lit up. He looked like a different person.

'But Steiner tells me you were forced into coming,' said Finn. 'Are you sure you wouldn't rather go home, lad?'

Lewis couldn't speak. He just shook his head and looked questioningly at us three. I managed a smile and Elliot gave him a thumbs-up sign, but Tara just looked coldly at him then turned away.

If Finn noticed the awkwardness, he didn't show it. So Lewis has a good heart, I thought. Then why had I spent so much time hating him? Then I caught Finn winking at Steiner. Was the whole mind-reading thing a hoax?

'What about me and Adam?' said Elliot.

Finn laughed. He came over and placed his hands on my head. It was very relaxing and I almost fell asleep.

'Hmm,' he said at last. 'A coward mind, but a brave heart . . . listen to your heart, Adam, and you'll be OK.'

'Only OK?' I thought, feeling really hurt. Then I saw Finn exchange another laughing glance with Steiner and I decided that the whole thing was a con trick.

'Do you want a turn, Tara?' said Finn.

'No thank you,' said Tara politely. 'I don't believe in this sort of rubbish.'

'Very wise,' said Liz.

'I'll have a turn,' said Elliot.

Finn laid his hands on Elliot's small head, and as he did so the smile left his face. It was the only time I ever saw this happen.

'Does this young one have to come on the mission?' he asked Steiner.

'There are three young McCoys, Finn,' said Steiner. 'Their IDs are linked in Rigg's system. It would look odd if one went missing.'

'I see,' said Finn, but he looked extremely worried.

Elliot, of course, couldn't see Finn's face.

'What's the verdict?' he asked.

'The verdict is, you're a great lad,' said Finn, but there was a look of real fear on his face. I was alarmed.

Meanwhile, Liz switched on the funny-looking kettle, sliced up a lemon and started making mugs of hot chocolate and tea. While the others were helping themselves, I took Finn's arm and steered him over to the table. There were paper and pens there and I took a sheet and wrote:

'*Why did you look scared?*

Finn hesitated, then in strange, looping writing he wrote:

'*I see danger for Elliot.*'

'*What from?*' I wrote.

'*Somebody with owl eyes.*'

'*Are you serious?*' I scribbled. '*Are you sure?*'

'*Yes,*' he wrote, and he underlined the word.

Then he crossed it out and wrote '*No. Not sure. Sorry.*'

I looked at him helplessly. He put a hand on my shoulder and whispered.

'Look after your brother and he'll be safe. Just watch out for those owl eyes.'

'OK,' I said and I scrumpled up the paper. I decided that Finn was barking mad. If you could invent time travel, then you were a total genius and it's well known that most of them are crazy. Look at Einstein – he couldn't even find his own house – and he wouldn't wear socks, even in winter, just in case they got holes in. There was no doubt about it, Finn was majorly insane.

'Be careful with that kettle, Liz,' he shouted. 'I'm not sure I've got the temperature control quite right.'

'I will be,' she said, holding it at arm's length and pouring boiling water into the mugs and cups. 'I haven't forgotten the fireworks you did for my birthday.'

'I can't have a reppy up here, you see,' he said to me. 'So I rigged up something like an electric kettle from your day. I'm pretty pleased with it.'

As he spoke, there was a bang and a bright flash from the kettle and Liz jumped back.

'That's interesting,' said Finn. 'Now why would that happen after switch off?'

Liz rolled her eyes at us and handed us each a mug of hot chocolate. Steiner had his tea black, in a proper teacup, with a slice of lemon. Finn didn't have hot chocolate or tea. He had his own flask, from which he poured himself a steaming mug of soup. It gave off a strong smell of fish.

I suddenly remembered the cans of Irn-Bru in my backpack.

'We brought these for you, Finn,' I said, handing him the two cans.

'Irn-Bru!' he shouted. 'My favourite. We used to drink this in the lab. I'll save it for a special occasion, thank you very very much.'

He placed the cans reverently on the table, then went to sit on his bed and slurp up the rest of his fishy soup. Steiner sat down next to him.

'A few words perhaps, Finn,' he said. 'To encourage the troops.'

Finn stood up and flung out his long grey arms.

'I am happy to meet you young people and I know you will succeed in your mission. If you need anything during your time here, I'll do my very best to help.'

'Thanks,' said Tara.

'In return I ask one special favour,' said Finn. 'It's about my sister Doll. She'd have loved to meet you four! She's fascinated by historical customs, you see. Her special interest is football fans and their songs.'

He sank down onto the bed.

'But I haven't seen her since last year when Rigg arrested her,' he went on. 'She's got a great mind, of course, and he put her to work in his labs. She can't have been very cooperative, because she's ended up in one of his underground prisons. We're the only two of our kind and you cannot imagine how much I miss her. So if you hear or see anything of Doll in London, please, please let me know.'

He put his face in his hands and began to cry. He was mad, but you couldn't help liking him. I wanted to cry too.

'I know how you feel,' said Lewis, speaking before the

rest of us had a chance. 'If your sister is alive, I promise I'll find her for you.'

'Does Doll like Irn-Bru too?' said Elliot, picking up one of the cans.

Finn lifted his smiling, tear-stained face and nodded.

'We'll take this then,' said Elliot. 'And give it to Doll when we find her.'

Liz reached out and ruffled Elliot's hair.

Then it all went rather quiet as we waited for Wilson to arrive. I felt the treehouse sway beneath us as the wind picked up and I watched Tara, who was writing a list on a Post-it note:

1. Get invitation from Stella.
   invite her to ours?
2. Find Doll
3. Ask reppy for things I've never had
   e.g. Baked Alaska
4. Find out how long I live

She caught me looking at her and crossed out the last item.

'Maybe not,' she said.

'What's keeping that Wilson?' said Steiner. 'He should be here by now.'

'Sshh,' said Tara. 'I think he's coming.' And we strained our ears to hear a faint, regular step coming up through the tree.

'At last,' muttered Steiner.

The climbing steps got louder. Then Wilson's head appeared through the hole in the floor. He had changed

into a black beret and combat gear, and as he climbed out,
I realised it wasn't Wilson at all. It was a young man.

I saw him reach for his holster . . . and bam!

6
Brainfeeds

The sound of my stun gun echoed round the treehouse. The young man lay slumped on the wooden floor, with a dart in the centre of his chest.

Lewis looked at me in astonishment and I heard Elliot dancing around behind me chanting:

'A-dam he's our man. If he can't do it no one can.'

What had I done? I turned around to Steiner in fear and panic, but he clapped me on the back.

'Well done Adam,' he said. 'He's a Rigg clone.'

'We-hey,' said Finn. 'Great shot! And the trigger didn't jam!'

'Brilliant,' said Tara softly.

A moment later, Wilson appeared. He collapsed on the cabin floor next to the drugged man. I felt sorry for him. He wasn't in great shape and he shouldn't have been climbing trees at his time of life.

'He followed me into the park,' panted Wilson.

'Careless,' tutted Steiner. 'You know the drill. You shouldn't come anywhere near Finn's place with a guard about.'

'I dived under a bush to hide,' said poor old Wilson. 'A holly bush, unfortunately. I thought he'd gone so I decided to press on. I was just opening up the tree when he dodged in front of me.'

Steiner shook his head disapprovingly. 'We'll have to make the best of it,' he said. 'But don't let it happen again, Wilson!'

'No harm done,' said Finn. 'I must say you've got some great recruits here, Steiner. Young Adam is a star – lightning reflexes.'

I felt a glow of pride. Tara patted me on the back. I looked round for Lewis, hoping that he'd heard, but he was busy examining the drugged guard. He found his ID card and read out the details.

'Rigg Clone 431: Istanbul.'

'Hmm,' said Finn. 'What's a Rigg clone doing out here in the sticks? You don't think someone tipped him off, Steiner?'

'Impossible,' said Steiner. 'The only people who knew we'd be here are myself, Wilson and Elizabeth.'

Liz lifted a curtain of camouflage vines to peer down out of the treehouse window.

'Can't see any more clones down there . . . and we should really head for the hovercar now, before it gets light.'

We said goodbye to Steiner and Finn and Lewis, who was helping to fix the kettle. Then we followed Liz and Wilson down the tree, through the park, along a dark, empty street and up a metal fire escape to the roof of a tall office building, where the hovercar was parked.

The sun rose as Liz set off north to London. Wilson dozed off, but we were wide awake, looking out at the other hovercars and the tall, flat-roofed buildings below us.

'I don't want to be rude,' said Elliot. 'But yours is a bit of an old crate compared to the other hovercars, isn't it?'

'It is,' said Liz. 'Finn lost ten prototypes trying to get back to your time. Steiner couldn't afford to let him use any more new models. But, as he says, this old banger will never get stolen by a Rigg clone.'

The time machine was a bit of a wreck. It was draughty and rusty, it rattled and its glass bubble was scratched all over. They kept it pretty messy too. I picked up a file of papers that had dropped out of the bag under Wilson's seat. It was labelled *OPERATION TIMEWARP* so I had a quick flick through. There were three sections headed *Recruitment, Undercover Operations* and *Results*, but I didn't have time to read them.

'You've found Steiner's file,' said Liz. 'Marvellous. Pass it over, darling, and I'll keep it safe. We wouldn't want it falling into the wrong hands.'

'Liz,' said Tara. 'What's the meaning of Istanbul?'

'It's the capital of Turkey,' I said smugly.

'That's Ankara, I think,' said Tara. 'What I meant was, why did it say Istanbul on that clone's ID card?'

'It's his name, petal,' said Liz. 'There are a thousand Rigg clones, you see. They just had numbers at first, but the nursery staff couldn't get on with that. In the end, they looked on an atlas site and gave them all the names of cities.'

'When do you think he'll wake up?' said Elliot.

'Hard to say, flower. The stun gun wears off pretty quickly, but Finn could always top him up with another sedative.'

'But what will they do when he does wake up?'

'They'll get him taken away before that, somewhere out of town probably.'

'But he'll get back some time,' said Elliot. 'And he'll tell about Finn's treehouse, won't he?'

'Don't worry, sweetie, Finn's probably left already. He's used to life on the run and he was planning to move to London anyway to find Doll.'

'They wouldn't . . . um . . . get rid of the clone?' I asked.

'How do you mean?'

'You know . . . waste him,' explained Elliot cheerfully. 'Take him out.'

'Kill him you mean? The dead men tell no tales approach? Absolutely not. We believe that every human life is sacred; a Rigg clone's as much as anyone else's. Steiner assured me that the mission would not involve any loss of life.'

I was pleased to hear it.

I was also pleased to be flying over London. We go up there once a fortnight to stay with our dad, so we know it pretty well. As we crossed the river, I saw that all the old landmarks were still there: the London Eye, the Houses of Parliament and Big Ben. There were no cars crossing the bridges though, and there were a lot of new, taller buildings, with flat roofs where the hovercars landed and took off.

'Where are we going?' asked Tara.

'Bickenhall Street,' said Liz.

'What's the nearest tube for that?'

'Baker Street,' said Liz. 'It's marvellous: less than a minute to the tube and handy for Regents Park and your new school. Which reminds me, you must start using the McCoys' names. We don't want any slip-ups in school on Monday.'

We already knew our new names. Tara's was Sky. Mine was Hunter and Elliot's was . . . Elliot. Maybe that was what caught Steiner's eye in the first place. We practised the names as we hovered slowly through the crowded skies of London. We looked so different, with our weird green eyes and shiny clothing, that the new names seemed to fit. I felt like a new man, with a new identity – Hunter McCoy.

Wilson woke up with a snort as the hover touched down on the roof of Bickenhall Mansions.

'Here already?' he said. 'You show them round, Liz, and I'll go and get Miss Trump.'

'Take care, Wilson,' said Liz, climbing out. 'See you later.'

'Who's Miss Trump?' said Sky, as we watched the hover go.

'She's the deputy head at your new school,' said Liz. 'She's with us. She's coming round later to give you some help with fitting in at school.'

We took the lift inside the building and Liz unlocked the door to our apartment, which was on the nineteenth floor.

'Welcome to Bickenhall Mansions,' she said, giving us all a perfumed hug. 'I can't wait to show you round.'

Our apartment had two floors. There were four enormous bedrooms on the top floor. The first one was Liz's and I glimpsed a clutter of flowers, clothes and makeup when she briefly opened the door. The next one was Sky's and the last two were for Elliot and me. Each bedroom had its own bathroom and each bathroom had one of those gigantic pipes they call flumes, sticking out of the wall. The flumes led down to the basement swimming pool and there was even a screen next to them, to show you who was down there before you took the plunge.

Liz showed us how to use the teeth-cleaning air jets and the auto-beds. Then we went downstairs and she explained the 3D projector in the sitting room and showed us the food replicator in the dining room and the rubbish and laundry chutes. We had a quick look in her study and ended up in the enormous games room, which had another food reppy, a snooker table, and a balcony.

When she'd shown us around, Liz gave us another hug.

'It's lovely to have you here and I don't like to leave you alone so soon,' she said. 'But I have to go to work now.'

'What do you do?' said Elliot.

'I'm a weather person.'

'On the telly?'

'That's right. You can watch me if you like: Channel 9 at 11.30.'

'Are you famous, then?' said Sky.

'D list,' said Liz.

We did watch her later. The projector was on the glass coffee table. At half-past eleven I asked it for Channel 9, and a little 3D Liz appeared, standing on the glass table on a 3D map wearing a shimmering golden dress. She told us it was going to be hot and sunny, and then she did an advert for sunscreen.

When it was over, Sky watched the soap that came next and I went out with Elliot onto the balcony. There were pots of blue roses growing out there and a table and chairs.

I picked one of the roses.

'I suppose you're going to give that to Sky?' said Elliot.

I ignored him. I tore off the delicate blue petals and let them fall over the balcony railings. We watched them flutter down into the street amongst the people walking and hovering far below. Like most streets, it was all pavement and there were two lines of trees and a fountain where the cars used to go.

'We could still be alive you know,' said Elliot. 'Down in those streets somewhere, very old and wrinkly.'

'Not you,' I said. 'You don't eat your five portions of fruit and veg.'

He was just about to jab me in the stomach when Sky came out.

'Talking of fruit and veg,' she said. 'Let's check out the reppy.'

It was a lot taller and shinier than the one in the garage, which had obviously been a very basic model.

'Do you think it does fish and chips?' said Elliot.

'I offer the full range of fish,' said the machine, in a deep male voice. 'I have cod, haddock, plaice, shark, crab, lobster, squid, vegetarian fish substitute . . . and much, much more.'

'I'll have cod and chips, please,' said Elliot.

'Me too,' I said.

'Make it three portions of cod and chips,' said Sky.

'Salt and vinegar on your chips?' said the machine.

We all nodded.

'Yes please,' said Elliot. 'And could we have some ketchup as well?'

Each portion of fish and chips came on a silver tray with a roll and butter, a wedge of lemon, a cotton napkin, a dish of ketchup, an after-dinner mint and a glass of sparkling water on the side. We took our trays out on the balcony and we'd just finished when the doorbell rang.

It was Wilson and our new deputy head, Miss Trump, was with him. She had cropped grey hair and a dark blue trouser suit with a cape like Steiner's. She was short and plump like Wilson and she looked rather nervous.

'This is Miss Trump,' said Wilson, without coming in. 'And these are our undercover agents. I'm terribly sorry but I must rush off now. Steiner needs me.'

Miss Trump looked alarmed to be left alone with us. She backed away, put down a huge pile of shopping bags, then put on a pair of round glasses and looked at us rather nervously.

'So you're the young people from the olden days,' she said weakly. 'You must be Sky,' she said with an effort. 'I'm very pleased to meet you.'

'And you,' said Sky, shaking her hand politely.

'And you must be Hunter,' she said to me, holding out her hand rather gingerly. 'How do you do?'

I've never really known the answer to that question, so I just said 'How do you do?' back and shook her hand.

'And young Elliot,' she said, reaching out and patting his head cautiously. 'Now, I've brought some clothes for you,' she said. 'But the real reason for my visit is your training. I suggest we do it in the largest room available.'

We showed her into the games room.

'You'll need to put these on,' said Miss Trump, taking three helmets out of a bag and handing them out. 'The teachers will have access to the real McCoys' school reports, so it's important you acquire all the skills they have.

'These are your brainfeeds,' she went on, giving us each a box of flexible coloured cards. The logo was the same on every one – *SkillFast: The Ultimate Brainfeed* – but the pictures and titles were all different. My cards had titles like this:

*SLAM DUNK complete basketball (introduced by
    Michael Jordan IV)*
MANDARIN CHINESE – Intermediate
*ADVANCED MATHS (Winner of the What Brain-
    feed Overall Prize 2099)*
RISE ABOVE IT – Meditation Techniques (Male)
*THE ART OF PERSUASION (Winner of the Life
    Skills Gold Prize 2098)*
DANCE CRAZY5 – Jive, Salsa and Tango
THE FAST LANE (racing strokes and dives)

My heart sank when I saw the swimming card. I couldn't swim and I hated deep water.

Miss Trump showed us how to use the brainfeed helmets.

'I'll need a volunteer to go first, so that you all know what to expect.'

Elliot shot his hand up.

'Thank you, Elliot. Which of your cards would you like to start with?'

'Total Chess,' he said.

That surprised me, because we didn't even have a chess set.

'Go ahead and tell us what you see.'

Elliot slotted the card into his helmet and put down his visor.

'Cool!' he said. 'Funky!'

'Tell us what you see, Elliot,' said Miss Trump patiently.

'I'm in a café,' he said. 'And there's a chess set in front of me. This man's come in. He's asking me what I want to learn . . . basic moves . . . opening gambits . . . something else . . . endgames . . . OK . . . I see.

'YES,' Elliot shouted. 'BASIC MOVES PLEASE . . . YES . . . READY.'

In an instant Elliot's hands and arms were a blur. They were jerking about all over the place snatching at the air. I thought he was having a fit and rushed to take off his helmet. Miss Trump caught hold of my shirtsleeve.

'Please leave him alone, Hunter,' she said. 'It's dangerous to disturb him during the brainfeed process. He's just practising the basic moves. He'll stop in a second.'

Sure enough he stopped.

Then he yelled 'OPENING GAMBITS PLEASE,' and he was off again. I'd never seen anyone's hands move so fast, not even a TV chef chopping an onion.

When he'd finished he slumped down on the sofa.

'Do my arms ache, or what? I feel like I've gone five rounds with Lennox Lewis.'

'But do you think it's taught you how to play chess, Elliot?' Sky asked, sitting down next to him.

'Yep,' he said nodding seriously. 'I think I'm a chess expert now. I could probably be in the England team.'

'For talking rubbish, maybe,' I said.

Elliot sprang up then and jabbed me in the belly. Just because I'm older than him, he thinks I'm impervious to pain. It's very annoying and I went to get him back, but Miss Trump looked at us in horror.

'Please stop that,' she said, clutching my arm. 'You really must make an effort to act like civilised human beings while you're here. You'll put me at risk if you behave violently at school.'

She looked genuinely upset. She sank down onto the sofa and put her head in her hands for a moment. Then she took a deep breath.

'I'm sorry,' she said. 'Let's get on. You can work at your own pace. I can see that it's going to be difficult for you two,' she said, looking at Elliot and me. 'But please try to be sensible. Brainfeeds stimulate brain, nerve and muscle activity. Some put a strain on the hands, the languages make your lips and face ache, and the physical subjects tax different parts of the body. You must take plenty of rests between cards. Remember, what you see is just virtual reality. You're still in the apartment. Be especially careful with the basketball, we don't want any broken bones,' she said nervously.

Off we went. If you'd seen us, you'd have thought we were loonies. Leaping up to catch imaginary balls, hands flailing with invisible objects, lips a blur and faces a picture of manic concentration.

I finished first, then Elliot.

Miss Trump had gone out onto the balcony to get some air and we sank down on the sofa, exhausted. Sky had taken more rests than us so she had lots of cards left to do. At that moment she was still hard at it – a whirling, spinning blur with a helmet on.

'Ballet,' said Elliot, with disgust, and he hobbled over to look at the brainfeed cards on the table.

'Look Hunter, there's stacks more cards in this other case. Hey! Cool! What about this one?'

I read the words on the card he passed to me:

'*HYPNOTIC POWERS. "If you want the mind powers of a Jedi Knight, this Feed's for you!" Indy Brainfeed March 2099 . . .*'

'Shall we try it, Hunter?'

'You bet,' I said, hurrying to put on my helmet.

A brainfeed is like a dream. It seems to last a long time, but in reality it's all over in seconds. Although you learn everything on it, you remember very little about how you did it. I don't recall much about the hypnosis brainfeed. I only know that VR people came up to me and I used a part of my brain I'd never used before to make them do things.

When it ended, I handed the card to Elliot. While he gabbled and flailed his way through it, I wondered whether the hypnosis would work on real people in real life.

Miss Trump came back in just as Elliot was taking his helmet off. He shoved the hypnosis card back in the case, but she eyed him suspiciously.

'I sincerely hope you haven't been taking in any of those cards there,' she said.

'No,' he said, crossing his fingers behind his back.

'I'm glad to hear it,' she said. 'They're bootleg cards I confiscated from a student. Pirate cards like these can be extremely dangerous and have even been known to cause permanent brain damage.'

Elliot did his cross-eyed idiot face while Miss Trump bent over to shut up the case, but he snapped out of it as she looked up at him sharply.

'Are you two taking a break?' she said.

'We've finished.'

'I can't believe you disobeyed my instructions. You can't have taken adequate rests. I insist that you relax completely now. Go on. Lie down on the sofas.'

We did as she said.

When I woke up I was stiff all over and I had a spectacularly painful headache. Elliot and Sky were asleep but Miss Trump was watching me rub my forehead.

'It's not safe to overstretch an underdeveloped mind,' she said, holding out a small red tablet in the palm of her hand. 'Take this, it'll sort that headache out.'

'I'm all right, thanks,' I said. Unfortunately, I couldn't help wincing as I spoke.

I didn't like talking to her, so I pretended to go back to sleep. Through half-closed lids I watched her move about the room. She went to the reppy and asked for a drink called Tranquilade. She downed it in one, then asked for another. Then she sat down and chewed at her nails. My head throbbed and I wished I'd taken her pill. Then an idea came to me. It was a bit scary so I put it into action straight away, before I could get cold feet.

I waited until she came over again. When she bent to look at me, through her big, round glasses, I opened my eyes wide and focused my mind onto hers as I'd learnt in the hypnosis brainfeed.

'Tell me the truth,' I thought. 'Why are you so nervous?'

Her face took on a dreamy look.

'I think Steiner's operation is a big mistake,' she said. 'It's exposing me and the school to unacceptable levels of danger.'

I was shocked.

'How come?' I thought.

'People are bound to notice you,' she said. 'You're uncivilised and disobedient and you and your brother jostle and fight like . . . cavemen.'

Cavemen? She was barmy. I was about to ask her if she was on our side at all, but I was interrupted by Liz coming in. I didn't want her to know I'd used the dodgy hypnosis card, so I focused one more thought on Miss Trump.

'Walk away from me and say hello to Liz.'

Then I did the triple blink to release her from the trance. If only I'd had more time. Miss Trump didn't seem to

56

be supporting us at all and I wasn't sure we should trust her. I decided to ask Steiner as soon as possible.

Meanwhile, it was time for the swimming. Miss Trump wouldn't let us use the flumes yet, so we went down to the pool in the lift.

I must have been looking scared, because Elliot squeezed my hand.

'You can do it, Hunter,' he whispered. 'It'll be over in no time. It's the perfect chance for you to learn.'

He was right of course. So why did I want to run away or use my new powers to hypnotise everybody back up to the safety of the flat?

'You've got to do it,' he said sternly. 'It could be important.'

The pool was completely empty; Liz had told us that everyone in our block went away at weekends. I don't re-member the swimming brainfeed. But I know I did it, because when I took my helmet off, my hair was dripping and every muscle in my body ached.

'You can do butterfly and back dives and everything,' said Elliot, excitedly. 'My brainfeed was shorter than yours so I watched you finishing off.'

Then Elliot did this amazingly high somersault into the water and proceeded to swim up and down like an Olympic champion.

'Come on Hunter,' said Sky, throwing off her towel. 'Let's show them the advanced stuff.' I really wanted to, but the old fear held me back.

I made some excuse about cramp and I sat and watched as Sky dived like a swallow into the water. She was wearing a red costume. She swam right under Elliot and her hair streamed behind her like weed. She caught hold of him and they went down in a tangle of arms and legs and came up laughing.

On the way back up in the lift Elliot was brimming over with excitement.

'You must be well pleased, Hunter!' he said.

I was – but how could I explain that I was still scared of deep water? Without the helmet on, I would never swim again; I was sure of it.

At least I'd got through it without making a fool of myself. I let Elliot's plans about the Great Britain swimming squad wash over me. I was thinking about what Miss Trump said. I'd told Elliot, but he was only interested in the success of the hypnosis.

'So that Jedi stuff really works,' he said excitedly. 'Amazing. We'll have no trouble with old Rigg now.'

Steiner turned up later on that evening, when we were all having supper, but when I finally got him on his own it was no better.

'I'm not sure we should trust Miss Trump,' I said.

Steiner raised his bushy white eyebrows and looked extremely annoyed:

'Whatever makes you think that, Hunter?'

'I took in a hypnosis brainfeed, the one that gives you Jedi powers.'

'What powers? What on earth are you talking about?'

'It was a brainfeed Miss Trump had. It gives you the mind powers of a Jedi Knight. You can get people to do and say things.'

'That's nonsense, Hunter. I've no idea what a Chedi Night is, but it sounds to me like one of those dodgy market-stall brainfeeds designed to part foolish people from their money. I shall tell Miss Trump to throw it away.'

'But it worked. I really did hypnotise Miss Trump and she told me how she thinks the mission is a mistake and that we're cavemen.'

'Now, now, Hunter, I can't believe that for one moment. Did this happen after this morning's brainfeed session?'

'Yes it did.'

'That explains it. Miss Trump told me you and Elliot disobeyed her clear instructions to take rests. What you experienced was a hallucination, caused by over-stimulation of the brain. Forget it. I trust Miss Trump absolutely and so should you.'

Steiner's comments left me confused. Was it really possible that I had imagined the whole thing?

Later on Miss Trump rang and asked to speak to Elliot and me.

'Steiner has just been reprimanding me for keeping pirate brainfeeds,' said her 3D image. 'I was so embarrassed. How could you lie to me like that?'

'We didn't want to worry you,' I said lamely.

'We didn't think it was important,' said Elliot.

'I'm very disappointed in you,' she said, shakily. 'You must promise to behave better at school. The teachers will expect complete cooperation and honesty.'

'OK.'

'And please don't imagine you have powers of hypnosis,' she said as her image disappeared. 'That silly brainfeed is a con. Everybody knows that.'

I was angry. They needed people who could tell lies, didn't they? That was the whole flipping point. I had a good mind to tell them to take their blasted mission and shove it. And I might have done too, if it hadn't been for the new clothes.

Apart from shoes and football boots, we didn't often get to choose new clothes from real shops. We mostly got our cousins' old stuff, or things from the market. So we were pretty excited about the huge pile of clothes Miss Trump had brought. It was like Christmas. There were leather boots, camouflage gear and cargo trousers and different coloured holsters for our stun gun mobiles. There were also funky fluid-filled watches with floating numerals, metal chains to hold our ID cards and these really cool wraparound shades. Then there were pyjamas, shirts and sports stuff – mostly made out of that fluid tinfoil material – in bronze, silver and gold.

Sky spent even more time trying clothes on than we did. When she finally emerged from her bedroom she was wearing a golden dress. It was tight down to her waist and then flared out in a skirt that shimmered as she moved.

'Hello boys,' she said, peering over her wraparound shades. 'How do I look?'

'Very nice,' said Elliot.

I had to agree.

'You look amazing, Tara – I mean Sky,' I said.

'You look cool too,' said Sky. 'You look like Zorro in those boots.'

Elliot made a puking noise, but I have to admit that I was pleased.

Sky showed us the rest of her stuff. She had more dresses in silver and metallic blue and green and loads of shoes, jewellery and bags. Some of the jewellery looked like real diamonds and you could tell she was really excited about it all.

But when Liz came back she frowned at Sky's golden dress and then demanded to see the rest.

'I knew I shouldn't have let Miss Trump organise the clothes,' she said. 'She has no idea. The boys' stuff will pass, but I'm afraid some of yours is way off, Sky. Nobody's gone for that girly look this summer. A young lady with enough money to go to Regents House School would have all the right things. We'll have to go shopping before you go out and meet anyone. You need more sports stuff and combat gear and different shoes. You also need a new haircut. Let's go tomorrow morning!'

'I'm afraid I haven't got any money for more clothes,' said Sky.

'Money's no problem, petal, the mission fund will pay.'

'Mission fund?' I said.

'Of course,' said Liz. 'Some very important people want Rigg out. How do you think we got this apartment? Isn't it fabulous? Have you tried out the flumes yet?'

'No,' said Elliot. 'Can we have a go now?'

'You're too late I'm afraid, darling, the pool closes at nine. Why don't you have a go tomorrow morning? We don't want men hanging around while we're shopping, do we, Sky? You two could stay here and have a proper swim while we get Sky something decent to wear.'

7
Diving Board and Flumes

Elliot was dead keen to try out his flume the minute he got up on Sunday morning.

'We haven't had any breakfast yet,' I warned him.

'Listen to yourself,' he said. 'You sound like Mum. I'll eat later.'

He began to root around in his cupboard for his silvery swimming shorts and wraparound goggles. Liz and Sky had already left for the shops and I went down to grab a quick breakfast from the reppy.

'I wonder if it does any kind of chocolate bar?' I said to myself.

'I can replicate Mars, Chompo, Felix, Hershey, Quadrant, Spiro, Sparx . . . and many more,' said the reppy. 'Please state your choice.'

'Um . . . Sparx, please,' I said. 'And a hot chocolate.'

When I opened the flap, there was a silver tray with a chocolate bar on a little plate, hot chocolate in a smart white and gold mug and three strawberries on the side.

'Yum,' said Elliot coming down the stairs. 'What's that?'

'A Sparx bar,' I said, munching away. 'It's lovely.'

'Maybe you were right about breakfast,' he said.

I liked the Sparx. Embedded in the chocolate were little see-through crystals of different colours. When you bit into them they fizzed and released different flavours . . . blackcurrant, liquorice and coke.

'I'm going to get one,' said Elliot. 'And a CloudNine, Liz said I should try it.'

The CloudNine bottle came with a tall glass. It was a nice big bottle, but the colour was cloudy grey.

'Yuck,' said Elliot. But when he poured it into the glass, it separated out into nine different brightly coloured layers.

'Funky,' said Elliot, sipping carefully from the first layer. 'Cherry . . . and that's lime . . . and that was strawberry . . . and that was pineapple . . . and something else fruity . . . and . . . I think I've had enough.'

He put down the glass, looking a bit queasy.

'I think I'll have my Sparx after the swim,' he said.

I followed him upstairs to his flume. He looked really small and skinny in his swimming stuff. For the first time I began to really worry about bringing him here.

'Excellent!' said Elliot looking at the empty pool in the screen next to his flume. 'You've just got to have a swim, Hunter. You're a new man now, you know.'

'Maybe,' I said, hoping that Hunter would rush in where Adam feared to tread, but I wasn't really bothered either way. I was just so pleased that I'd hypnotised Miss Trump. It meant I would be able to handle anyone at all. I hardly needed my stun gun, but I wore it just the same.

'Meet you down there,' said Elliot, launching off into his flume.

I went into my bathroom and looked at my green-eyed reflection in the mirror. I thought I looked pretty cool. Then I noticed that Elliot had stuck one of Sky's Post-it notes to it:

hunter mcsquish
can swim like a fish
but hes a wimp
and fat as a blimp
so there just isnt room
for him in his floom
he thinks hes cule with Jedi powres
but all he does is pick girls flowres

I am not fat, as it happens, but I did take the lift down to the pool because I still couldn't face swimming. When I got down there, Elliot was already splashing around. There was a great big beach ball in the corner, so I threw it hard at his head. Then I had a proper look around. There was a high diving board and a springboard, and the bottom of the pool was a sparkling mosaic of sea creatures made of tiny gold and blue tiles.

'You have got to ride the flume,' shouted Elliot, clambering out of the pool. 'It's wild. There's music and it gets dark.'

I watched him dive off the springboard. His legs were all crooked and there was a terrible smack when he hit the water, but he didn't seem to mind. Then he swam about, calling out for me to join him. The funny thing was, his swimming was rubbish.

I dared myself to climb up onto the high diving board. I

managed it, but I couldn't stand up. I stretched out flat on my back instead and watched the rippling waves of light on the ceiling. When I rolled over onto my front and looked over the edge of the board I saw two young men coming in through the glass doors.

They were both tall, with black hair and moustaches. They were armed too and my stomach churned as I realised they both looked exactly like the Rigg clone I'd shot at the treehouse. Elliot was staring at them in horror. I shrank back out of sight, keeping myself as flat as possible. One of the clones, who was wearing wraparound mirror shades, stripped down to his shorts and shades and jumped into the pool.

'Come on Stan,' he yelled. 'Let's teach him a lesson.'

I peered desperately over the edge of the diving board, staying low to keep out of sight. I got out my stun gun and tried to aim at Mirrors. It was a difficult angle and he kept moving, so I tried the hypnosis. I wanted to make him say: 'These are not the boys we are looking for.' But I couldn't make eye contact.

Mirrors swam over to Elliot, took his small head in his big hands and thrust it underwater. The other guard, Stan, was looking on from the side. Was it my imagination, or did he look disgusted?

'That's enough!' he shouted. 'He's not the one who shot me, anyway.'

'Who cares, Stan?' said Mirrors. 'I'm going to finish the little rat off. Then I'm going to have a nice long swim.'

Stan tore off his jacket angrily as though he was going to wade in too. I stood up to try to get a better shot. Stan must have heard me because he looked up. To my astonishment, he grinned at me and put up his arms in mock surrender. Then he leaned back against a pillar to watch.

Meanwhile Mirrors was still struggling with Elliot in the water. They were right underneath me now but I still couldn't get a clear shot at the clone. I took off my stun gun holster. Somehow I had to find the courage to jump from the high board into the deep water.

Elliot was weakening.

'Help!' he shouted, desperately. 'Please!'

Mirrors pushed him under again. Elliot wasn't even struggling any more.

I looked across at Stan. He was looking at me as if he knew me. Then, to my astonishment, he mouthed the words, 'Go for it!'

I jumped. I felt a rush of air and then my foot struck someone's head. I sank right down into the horrible deep water with Mirrors underneath me. When I surfaced again, the clone was at the bottom of the pool. Elliot was half underwater and the mirror shades were floating about on their own. I grabbed Elliot and managed to swim to the steps, towing him along with me. He didn't seem to be breathing. I was dimly aware of the clone called Stan diving into the pool, but I knew I had to concentrate on Elliot. I put him in the recovery position and I started to give him the kiss of life, like I learnt in first aid. I'm not very confident about things like that, but I just did my best. It seemed to go on for a long time. I was dimly aware of Stan leaving through the glass doors, carrying a body, but I knew I still had to concentrate on Elliot. Finally, his chest started to rise and fall on its own, like it's supposed to. He sat up and coughed.

'Thanks,' he spluttered.

It was great to hear his voice. I looked around with tears in my eyes. We were alone again; the clones were nowhere to be seen. There was nothing underwater, only the mirror shades floating on the surface. I fished them out.

'They've gone,' said Elliot.

'I think one of them might have drowned,' I said. 'He was on the bottom and I think I saw the other one dive in and drag his body out.'

'He'll report us.'

'I'm not so sure about that,' I said. Then I explained how the one called Stan had grinned at me and mouthed the words 'Go for it'.

'Weird,' said Elliot. 'And he said something about us shooting him. What was the name of the guard in the treehouse?'

'Istanbul,' I said, leaving Elliot for a moment to go and retrieve my stun gun from the diving board.

When I got back down he was looking thoughtful.

'Istanbul's got Stan in it. Could it be the same bloke?'

'You can't tell. They all look the same. Anyway, I shot him. Why would he want to help me?'

Elliot shrugged.

When we got back upstairs, I changed into dry clothes. I got Elliot a hot chocolate and made him wrap up warm and get into bed. He wouldn't stay there long though, because he wanted to destroy the evidence of the mirror shades. He used Liz's candle lighter thing to melt them into a pool of sticky plastic. I opened the windows, but it still made a terrible stink.

'Those shades were the problem,' I said. 'I tried to hypnotise that clone, but I don't think it works when you can't make eye contact.'

'It wasn't just that,' he said glumly. 'I tried it on the other one too, but I don't think it works when you're in a panic.'

That was a blow. I realised we were way out of our depth. In our other life we sometimes had a bit of hassle from Lewis. That seemed like a big deal at the time, but here we were having to deal with attacks from armed men – on a daily basis.

When Sky and Liz came back we told them everything. Liz's face fell.

'If that clone Stan reports you to Rigg, we're done for.'

'Not necessarily,' said Elliot. 'You heard what Hunter said about Stan. What's he going to say when they ask him why he stood and watched while his clone brother drowned? I'm pretty good at excuses myself, but that would take some explaining.'

'Elliot's right,' said Sky. 'That Stan guy won't say a word.'

'But what will he do with the body?' I said. 'If he did drown.'

'That's his problem,' said Elliot. 'Can we have some lunch now, Liz? I'm starving.'

'Help yourself,' said Liz, laughing. 'You're cool customers, I'll give you that. I'm going out right now to tell Steiner, though. You may be right about that Stan, but it's still a very serious matter.'

'Why don't you ring him?' said Sky.

'If Rigg is onto us, they might be listening in on my calls.'

So Liz went out, telling us not to let anyone into the flat while she was gone.

Sky was in a very good mood. She'd enjoyed her shopping. We got her a CloudNine from the reppy and she loved it. Then she ordered some top pizzas for us with loads of nice things on, followed by baked Alaska, which turned out to be an amazing cake with hot meringue on the outside and cold ice cream on the inside.

'How does it do that?' said Elliot.

'Dunno,' said Sky. 'I've never had it before. Lewis's granny asked me if I'd like it on my birthday. I think I'll say yes.'

'Wonder how old Lewis is getting on?' I said.

'Probably been blown up by Finn's kettle,' said Elliot.

'I wish,' said Sky.

Then she showed us all her new stuff. There were millions of bags and a large cardboard box. She wanted us to guess what was inside it.

The box moved a little. I put my ear to it and heard scratching and panting.

'Some GMO thingy?' said Elliot.

'A two-headed cat?' I said.

'Open it and see,' said Sky.

Inside was a fluffy white dog, a little bit like the one in the Tintin books. He looked up at us all with soft brown eyes.

'Hello Snowy,' said Elliot, reaching in and scratching his ears. Snowy's tail thumped the side of the box.

'Wilson bought him for us,' said Sky. 'We met him on Oxford Street. Wilson said we were under a lot of pressure and dogs are good for stress. He thought a dog would take the edge off our homesickness and the worry of the mission and everything.'

I thought that was very kind of Wilson, and he was right, Snowy was terrifically relaxing. He liked having his head scratched. He had a really waggy tail, he was a great jumper and he could catch a small ball in his mouth. If you were feeling a bit lonely, or cold, he'd come and sit on your lap and warm you up. We played with him for ages.

Sky showed us the beanbag bed she'd chosen for him. It was blue with yellow bones on. Snowy padded round and round on top of it until he'd made a comfortable nest. Then he settled down for a nap.

Then Sky wanted to show us her new clothes. She went to put on her favourite outfit, which was called a catsuit. It was metallic, with colours that changed as she moved. Her hair was shinier and straighter than Tara's used to be, because of the new haircut. It swished to and fro each time she moved her head. Her green eyes looked amazing too. I thought she looked fantastic, and I might even have said so, except that we suddenly heard the unmistakable sound of the front door opening. Then slow footsteps that definitely were not Liz's.

We all froze. Sky grabbed Snowy and Elliot and vanished behind the long trailing curtains. I ducked behind the door, with my stun gun ready.

'Where in heaven's name are you?' said a worried voice. It was Miss Trump.

We stepped out and Snowy dashed round her in circles barking and wagging his tail.

'He's called Snowy,' said Elliot. 'Wilson got him for us.'

Miss Trump patted him gingerly on the head.

'I had to see you urgently,' she said. 'SkillFast has issued a warning about those swimming brainfeeds. Apparently the learning effect only lasts a few minutes. They've sent me replacement cards with the fault corrected. I hope you haven't been swimming. If you were non-swimmers before, you could easily have drowned!'

Maybe that's what you wanted? I thought. I was beginning to get suspicious. First there was the ladder thing, then the clone turning up at the treehouse, then the clones at the pool and now this. Somebody was up to no good.

Then I was struck by a great thought. If the brainfeed hadn't worked, that meant I had managed to swim on my own!

'I knew there was something wrong with the way you were swimming, Elliot,' I said. 'Because I don't remember seeing a beginner's belly-flop and doggy-paddle card.'

He took a flying leap at me then and knocked me to the ground. I bashed my head on the polished floor, which was a bit painful, so I lay there groaning and laughing, with Snowy licking my face.

'Oh my goodness, they're at it again,' said Miss Trump, peering nervously down at me. 'Please get off the floor and be normal.'

I stood up and brushed myself down.

'Thank you,' she said, taking a deep breath. 'Let's go down and retake the brainfeeds right away.'

She wrote a note for Liz.

'I'll stick it on the hall mirror,' she said. 'That way she's bound to see it.'

Miss Trump said she'd meet us down at the pool. We left Snowy on his beanbag with a couple of reppy dog biscuits. Then we went to our bathrooms and changed.

'5-4-3-2-1 . . . Thunderbirds are go!' yelled Sky from her bathroom.

'F.A.B.,' said Elliot.

Ignoring my lurch of fear, I launched myself into the flume. Bickenhall Mansions was a twenty-storey building, stretching the whole length of the street. My flume must have weaved its way round every single apartment in the block. There was music playing in the tube; I think it was the theme tune from *Indiana Jones*. Down I went, hurtling along, sometimes in the dark. I had enough time to try sitting up and lying down and swaying in time to the music. It went on so long that I began to fear that it might be a trap. Then suddenly, I came out into the blue light of the basement pool and flew through the air into the warm water . . . at exactly the same time as Sky. Elliot's skinny body came flying out of his tube a few seconds later.

'What a ride!' he shouted.

We got out and Miss Trump passed us the brainfeed helmets. When it was over, I dived in with the other two to try out our stylish new strokes. It was brilliant.

Miss Trump said goodbye to us downstairs. We wrapped ourselves in the huge white towels that were piled up down there. Then we took the lift back up to the nineteenth floor. Steiner and Wilson were there having a cup of tea with Liz.

Steiner stood up formally to shake our hands.

'We've heard all about the unfortunate incident at the pool and you're not to worry about it,' he said graciously. 'Wilson has been running around town for me talking to his sources. The word is that both clones have gone missing: AWOL. They're not the first clones to disappear. We don't know what that Stan is up to, but I don't think we'll be hearing from him again.'

'Marvellous,' said Liz. 'Now why don't you all go upstairs and change? Shove the towels down the laundry chutes, then come down and have a drink with us.'

As I followed Sky upstairs, I looked at her wet hair dripping on her bare shoulders. It reminded me of something that had been worrying me:

'You know we're supposed to be brother and sister?' I said.

'Yes,' she said, looking round and smiling.

'Well, we don't look alike, do we . . . it's not possible.'

'He's right,' said Elliot. 'We're not even the same colour.'

'I know what you mean,' said Sky. 'I asked Liz about it and she says it's cool. She said people have messed about so much, choosing skin and hair colour, that you get all sorts of combos . . . nobody notices.'

So that was OK.

When we came down again we got mugs of hot chocolate and flopped on the sofas. Snowy came bounding in from the other room and jumped up onto Elliot's lap.

He padded round and round on him for a bit, then curled up and went to sleep.

'Thanks for giving us Snowy, Wilson,' I said.

'Yes,' said Sky. 'He's great.'

'You're very welcome,' said Wilson, smiling through his round tinted glasses.

'I wanted to have a word with you about that dog, Wilson,' said Steiner, who was walking towards the study, clutching his Operation Timewarp file. 'I can't see a real problem with it, but I must insist that you consult me before you make any more unilateral decisions that could affect the security of the mission.'

'The little dog just caught my eye,' said Wilson, apologetically. 'I'm sorry I didn't consult you. It won't happen again.'

'See that it doesn't,' said Steiner and he went into the study, closing the door behind him.

'What is he like?' said Sky. 'Doesn't he ever get on your nerves, Wilson?'

Wilson looked startled.

'No, no,' he said. 'Steiner's a great man, a visionary. I'm proud to work for him.'

He changed the subject by turning to Snowy.

'Are they looking after you properly, boy?' he said, bending down to scratch behind Snowy's ears.

Snowy barked once.

'Giving you good healthy food, are they? Not too many doggy-chocs, I hope. We don't want you getting fat, do we?'

Snowy said nothing.

'Take him out with you whenever you can,' said Wilson to Elliot. 'He needs a good long run every day.'

Steiner and Wilson stayed all evening. We had a game of pool, and I got us some sweet and sour pork with special fried rice from the games room reppy. Then we joined the adults and sat in drowsy silence while they talked. As I listened to the hum of voices, my eyes grew heavy.

'We can congratulate ourselves on our recruits. The lads showed great courage down at the pool . . . and the girl is extremely bright, she'll have no problems making friends with Stella Rigg. We've been lucky with that Lewis too. Finn says he's a diamond . . . willing and very able . . . he can go to all the places where Finn daren't show his face . . . it's looking good . . .'

I opened my eyes to see that Elliot was fast asleep, so I forced myself awake and helped him upstairs to bed. It was school in the morning.

8
At School

Regents House School was for people aged five to sixteen. I was in the same class as Sky, but Elliot was on his own. He was a bit nervous about it.

'My name's Elliot McCoy,' he rehearsed, on the way to school. 'I live with my Aunt Liz. My mother won the lottery and she's having cosmetic surgery. Yikes. They're going to tease us about that, aren't they Hunter?'

'Maybe, but we don't care, do we? We don't even know her. Nothing they say about us will hurt. Because it's not really us, is it?'

Elliot thought about that for a bit.

'Cool,' he said. 'But we're new aren't we, they'll pick on us.'

'Maybe a little,' I said. 'But there won't be any real bullies, Elliot, because people aren't rough any more . . . only the Rigg clones . . . not the ordinary people.'

Elliot thought about that too.

'Cool,' he said again.

Regents House School was in one of those enormous white houses you get in London. Miss Trump was sitting at the reception desk. She looked pretty nervous when she saw us arrive, and buried her head in her papers. We had been told to ignore her, because we weren't supposed to have met her yet. I was happy to comply.

We took Elliot upstairs to his classroom first and Sky gave him a hug before he went in. I felt for him, but he gave us a quick thumbs-up sign and went straight in.

There were only ten people in our class: five boys and five girls. I had a good look at Stella Rigg. Funnily enough, she was the only one who didn't have those green eyes. She didn't look like a tyrant's daughter. She had shiny brown hair, blue eyes and a nice smile, and she was happy to let Sky sit next to her. Mind you, who wouldn't be?

We had the usual old subjects on the timetable, like Languages, Maths, Science and English, but we also had some different ones. There was Relaxation, which stopped you getting stressy. There was Verbal Skills, which taught you how to talk other people into doing stuff. There was also Creativity, which was art, music, dance, drama and lots more, depending on your personality profile. Of course, the profiles they had for us weren't really ours at all. I was down for sculpture, but I only finished one thing. It was supposed to be a Greek discus thrower, but as Sky said, it looked more like Homer Simpson eating a pizza. Maybe the real Hunter McCoy would have done better.

I'd been wondering what we'd actually do at school, because of the brainfeeds being so effective. But it turned out that the brainfeeds just gave you the basics. Lessons were a chance to experiment and apply what you'd learnt. Everyone was a boff at maths, so there were no sums to do. The lessons were your chance to work as a team to use the maths to solve problems. That was the theory anyway, but Alice Ho and AJ Sherif were the only two in our class who had any really good ideas, so the rest of us just tagged along with them.

In the same way, everyone was an ace swimmer, so there were no races. The lessons were an opportunity to create synchronised swimming routines with the rest of your class. Synchronised swimming! That was typical of sport at that school. There was no football or anything. There was a room where you could play squash and table tennis against a virtual reality opponent . . . but I didn't get round to trying that. In the group PE lessons, we just did dance, Tai Chi, gymnastics and a very controlled form of basketball. I must admit that I got to like the dancing, because they had some really funky music, and once you'd done the brainfeed you were a wicked dancer. The basketball was OK too, but if you shoved someone just a little bit, trying to get the ball, they blew the whistle and seemed very shocked. We learnt to be very careful.

In some ways it was easy to get on with people at that school. Nobody hassled us. Nobody called us the McGeeks or anything, even though we were new. In other ways it wasn't so easy. Elliot took in a load of Sparx bars one day and offered them round at playtime. Only Stella took one. The others all said no; they'd been taught not to eat sweet things between meals, you see.

I can still remember the register in our class:

Storm Abraham
Roshan Bapoo
Alice Ho
Marc Marquez
Hunter McCoy
Sky McCoy
Aurora Price
Venus Price
Stella Rigg
AJ Sherif

Alice and AJ were the cleverest. Marc was the most annoying, though Sky seemed to like him all right. The Price twins were too shy even to speak to us, but none of them were what you'd call sociable, so there weren't many laughs at all. The one exception was Stella, luckily for us. She was a bit of an airhead, but she was friendly and fun.

There was a games room at school and you could book a slot there at lunchtime. The games used helmets and the same virtual reality technology as brainfeeds. I had a go at the most popular game, Treasure Hunt. In one level you were in an Egyptian pyramid and you ran around looking for jewels and things. It was very realistic and quite good fun, but I wasn't hooked. There was no fighting in it and no feeling of fear or danger. They'd also ruined it with this educational stuff. Just when you were getting into it, this character would appear and get you to read a scroll before you could pass him. Elliot tried a Ju-Jitsu move on him, but he just got Game Over and an electronic warning from the network.

Another thing that annoyed Elliot was the school meals. Liz didn't really notice what we ate, any more than she noticed when we went to bed. We could have fish and chips for breakfast and ring doughnuts and hot chocolate at midnight. But it wasn't quite like that at school. We discovered that on our very first day, when we arranged to meet up with Elliot in the lunch hall.

'Chips, three sausages . . . a jam doughnut and a chocolate milkshake, please,' said Elliot happily.

A red light came on.

'Warning,' said the machine. 'You have made a low-vitamin, high-fat selection. Please try again.'

Elliot's face fell.

'Pants,' he said. 'The one in the flat never says that. What shall I do, Hunter?'

He looked at me for advice, but I couldn't help. I didn't want to say the wrong thing in front of all those school people.

Elliot thought for a very long time.

'Chips, two sausages . . . a jam doughnut, a chocolate milkshake and an orange juice please.'

The red light stayed on.

'Warning,' said the machine. 'You have made a high-fat selection. Please try again.'

'That is so tight,' said Elliot, much too loudly. 'Orange juice is well healthy.'

'Sshh,' I said.

Somebody tapped me on the shoulder. My heart sank; it was Stella Rigg.

'Didn't you have a wise-options reppy at your last

school?' she asked me. 'I thought they were compulsory.'

I just shrugged and smiled.

'There's no way a wise-options will let you have chips and sausages and a doughnut,' she said to Elliot.

'No?'

'No. Way too high in fat.'

'I don't care about that,' said Elliot, showing her his skinny arm. 'Look how thin I am . . . and I'm always eating chips and stuff . . . and Big Macs.'

'Big whats?' she said.

I kicked Elliot to make him shut up. He glowered at me.

'Just choose something healthy,' I whispered. 'People are looking.'

Elliot was rubbing his leg resentfully. I backed off. He looked as if he might thump me – then everybody would know that we weren't what we seemed.

Sky stepped between us.

'Why not drop the chips and the doughnut, Elliot, and just have sausage and salad?' she said gently.

'No way,' he said. 'I do not eat raw leaves.'

'Chicken and chips then?'

'All right,' he said gloomily, turning back to the machine. 'Chicken and chips and orange juice and a chocolate milkshake please.'

'Please add a vegetable or salad to your selection,' said the machine.

Elliot sighed deeply.

'Chicken and chips and peas and orange juice and a chocolate milkshake.'

'What's the magic word?' said the machine.

For one horrible moment I thought Elliot was going to kick it. There was a queue of people behind us now and some of them were giggling nervously. Elliot turned and glared at them and they fell silent.

'Please,' he said, with dignity.

A green light came on and Elliot lifted the flap to get his tray.

'Yuck,' he said. 'Those squidgy peas . . . and they're squashed under the chips . . . I really hate it when that happens.'

He trudged off to an empty table, over by the window, and started to pick miserably at his food.

Sky got her first choice: tuna and rice salad, a bread roll and a yogurt. Then she stood and grinned, watching me make three attempts before I got the green light for pepperoni pizza and green beans.

'Cheer up,' said Sky softly, sitting down next to Elliot. 'It'll do you good to eat some veg.'

Elliot gave her a look of scorn.

'I eat loads of veg.'

'Yeah, right.'

'I do.'

'Like what?'

'Like beans . . . chips . . . tomatoes . . . well, ketchup anyway . . . and I eat fruit.'

'Chocolate oranges, maybe,' said Sky, taking a big bite out of her roll.

I was too nervous to eat. I just sat and watched the steady stream of hovercars passing outside the high windows.

'They're starting to notice we're different, aren't they?' I said.

'Nonsense,' said Sky, smiling round calmly at the other tables. 'But they will if you keep acting weird. You're chewing on your fork. Put it down. Try to look normal.'

I did my best, but as I watched Elliot hiding his peas in his pocket, I began to feel more and more anxious for him. They were bound to find him out at this school. Though he seemed quite at home, polishing off the rest of his food and waving cheerily at a tall figure heading for our table.

'Hello Mr Slater,' he said.

It was Elliot's class teacher.

'Could you come to Miss Trump's office for a moment, Elliot,' said Mr Slater. 'I want to have a quick word with her about you.'

I didn't know what to do. There wasn't time to try the Jedi stuff. I could only watch in horror as Elliot stood up and followed him out of the cafeteria.

9
Down the Tubes

We waited in the cafeteria for ages. Everyone else left, but Elliot still didn't come back. The bell rang and I raced up to his classroom to see if he was there. I hovered by the doorway watching all the other eight-year-olds filing in. Then Mr Slater arrived and he gave me a really suspicious look.

'Why are you chewing a fork?' he said.

'I'm looking for my brother,' I said, stuffing the fork in my pocket.

'He's still with Miss Trump, I'm afraid.'

'Can you tell me why?'

'I suggest you ask Elliot later,' he said and he closed the classroom door gently, but firmly, in my face.

I pegged it down the stairs to Miss Trump's office. I was just summoning up the courage to knock on the door when it opened and Elliot came out.

'Thank God you're safe,' I said, flinging an arm round him. 'What's the problem?'

'Get off,' he said. 'The only problem is you freaking out for no reason. They just want to know if I'm willing to represent the school in a chess tournament. Apparently the real Elliot McCoy is a top chess boff . . . just like me.'

'So everything's all right, then?' I said with relief.

'It would be if you could just chill out,' he said and I followed him as he ran back upstairs to the classrooms.

We walked back together from school that night. You didn't have to worry about traffic, but you had to watch your back sometimes because of all the hoverboards. Marc Marquez zoomed past us on his. He did a smart little turn when he saw us and swung back to hover alongside Sky.

'Hi Sky,' he said, ignoring Elliot and me. 'Did you like your first day at Regents House?'

'Yes, thanks Marc,' said Sky.

'I'm glad,' he said, shooting off and smiling back at her over his shoulder. 'Look forward to seeing you tomorrow.'

'What a creep,' I said, hoping he would slam into a wall.

Elliot was looking after him admiringly.

'Do you think Aunt Liz would get us hoverboards?' he said, hopefully.

'She might do,' said Sky. 'She didn't mind spending a fortune on my clothes.'

We were interrupted by a loud bleeping noise.

'What the flip is that?' I said.

'It's your mobile, you wally,' said Elliot. 'Why don't you answer it?'

So I did.

'Waassupp?' said a familiar voice.

'Is that Lewis?' I said.

'You shouldn't use my name on the phone,' said Lewis.

'Is that the legendary skateboard wizard of West End Close, then?'

He ignored me.

'We've got to meet up,' he said. 'I think I've found something important.'

'What?'

'I can't say. Meet me tonight at nineteen hundred hours, outside Warren Street tube . . . if you can find it.'

'Of course we can find it.'

'And don't keep me hanging around . . . OK?'

I said nothing. I was working out nineteen hundred hours.

'OK?' he repeated.

'OK,' I said reluctantly, and the connection went dead.

'Was that Lewis?' said Elliot.

I nodded. 'He wants us to meet him tonight at seven. He reckons he's found something important.'

'Oh yeah?' sniffed Sky. 'Like that great lump could even find a tin of beans in Tesco. You two can meet him if you like, I'm going to stay in and wash my hair.'

I didn't argue with her. I'd once spent half an hour looking for beans in a supermarket myself. I was quite looking forward to seeing old Lewis again. He was a very annoying person, but at least he wouldn't treat you like an axe murderer just because you pushed someone in a basketball match.

We saw Lewis before he saw us. He was wearing camouflage gear. He'd lost his slouch and acquired a swagger.

Elliot put a hand on his shoulder and Lewis turned round.

'Good to see you,' I said – and I think I half meant it.

'Where's Tara?' he said.

'Sky, you mean,' I said. 'She's washing her hair.'

'Oh yeah?' he said. 'Follow me, then, but keep your distance.'

Elliot made a face at me as Lewis swaggered off down the Tottenham Court Road. We waited a minute then hurried after him. He went down a side street, and then dodged down a narrow cul-de-sac and an even narrower alleyway, past the fire escapes of tall office buildings. He went through a metal door at the end, which clanged shut behind him. We opened the door and found ourselves in a kind of warehouse, with a dirty concrete floor. It was empty except for an old wooden crate in one corner.

'Where on earth is he?' said Elliot.

I shrugged my shoulders. 'There must be another way out.'

Then we both jumped as the metal door clanged shut behind us. The only light came from a single skylight in the roof and it was just enough to see by. Elliot went round looking at all the walls, then inside the wooden crate.

'Over here, Hunter,' he said, and he jumped into the crate and disappeared.

I went over and saw that the crate concealed an entrance to a steep spiral staircase. Elliot was climbing down it and I followed him. The spiral steps went on and on . . . and on. At last we reached the end and we staggered, dizzy and trembling, onto a familiar-looking platform. In the dim light we could just make out the white lines painted on the platform edge and the piles of rubble where the walls had caved in. Lewis was there waiting and shining a torch at an ancient peeling poster on the wall.

It seemed to be an advert for an electric car.

'Where are we?' said Elliot.

'In an old tube station, of course,' said Lewis. 'They don't use the Northern line any more; it's too dangerous. But it's Finn's secret passageway in and out of town. You'll need these,' he said.

There were four hoverboards in a pile on the old platform. He handed one to each of us.

'Wow! Thanks, Lewis,' said Elliot happily.

'Are they for us to keep?' I asked.

Lewis nodded.

'They're not new, but they work all right. Finn's got loads of them, he was using them for one of his experiments.'

Hoverboards are much thicker than skateboards, but lighter. The tops are white and textured and the undersides have the brand name and a design. Ours were both FlyBoys. Elliot's had a red and gold dragonfly on an orange background and mine had a little green alien on dark blue. It was a bit battered, but it was the best thing I'd ever been given.

There are lights on the front and back of a hoverboard and turbo vents at each end. It's important not to cover the vents with your feet, because that stops the air flowing through and you can't hover. I turned mine over and over, examining every part.

'Finn's very generous, isn't he?' said Elliot. 'Has he made you a stun gun yet?'

'He hasn't had time,' said Lewis. 'So he gave me an early prototype. I can't use it, because it backfires. I spent half yesterday unconscious.'

I tried not to laugh but it just burst out.

'Come on,' said Lewis, suddenly impatient again. 'This place gives me the creeps . . . and I want you to hear what I heard.'

He zoomed off down the dark tube tunnel with the fourth hoverboard under his arm. He turned and faced us, hovering in mid-air.

'Hurry up!' he yelled.

We'd watched other people on their hoverboards, so we knew exactly what to do. We stamped on them to start them, then shoved off quickly and raced wildly down the dark tunnel after Lewis. The air was cool and dusty as it rushed against our faces and our board lights lit up old posters and cracked tiles as we flashed past another abandoned station. Soon we'd overtaken Lewis. We saw a bright light up ahead and we zoomed towards it.

'Slow down!' Lewis shouted. 'Stop. Stop now!'

I heard the panic in his voice and stamped my foot again to stop, swerving to a curving halt and grabbing Elliot's shirt just in time, as a high-speed tube train streaked across our path. We had come to a point where a working tube line crossed the disused Northern Line.

'Sorry Lewis,' I said.

'I forgot what morons you were,' he grinned. 'I would have warned you, but I thought you'd realise what the lights meant.'

We hovered slowly after that, shoulder-to-shoulder,

three abreast. We stopped at the next old station and landed lightly on the platform.

'We've got to be dead quiet now,' said Lewis. 'Leave your boards here and come and listen.'

He led us to the far end of the platform where the tattered remains of an old Gap poster smiled across at us over the empty tracks. Elliot started to rattle the drawer of an ancient chocolate machine, but Lewis asked him to step aside and he lifted the whole machine right off the tiled wall. Then he pressed his ear against a ventilation grille, which was revealed in the crumbling tiles. He motioned to us to do the same. At first I heard nothing but the hum of distant trains. Then I heard a sigh and a woman's voice singing *You'll Never Walk Alone* in a Scottish accent.

Before we could stop him, Elliot joined in. I clapped my hands over Elliot's mouth, but it was too late. The woman behind the wall had heard.

'Who's there?' she called.

There was a pause, and then we heard a man shouting:

'Are you talking to someone in there? Have you made yourself a mobile? Answer me, you freak!'

There was silence.

'OK. Don't talk to me,' said the menacing voice. 'But I'm warning you . . . if you are communicating with anyone outside you are in serious trouble. Go and stand in the hall. I'm searching your cell.'

There was the sound of a scuffle, then a lot of banging and scraping.

'He might look through the grille and see us,' whispered Elliot. 'Let's get out of here.'

Lewis nodded. He carefully hooked the old chocolate machine back on its rusty brackets, then we crept back to the boards and cruised back to the previous station. We sat down on the old platform with our legs dangling over the edge, watching mice scuttling in and out over the old tracks.

'Who do you reckon that was, then?' said Lewis.

'She sounded Scottish,' I said.

'Yes, like Finn,' he said. 'It's his sister Doll, isn't it? He said she was into football songs.'

'Cool!' said Elliot.

'How on earth did you find her, Lewis?' I said.

'Finn heard she was in an underground prison some-where,' he said. 'He's been listening out for her at all the abandoned stations, but he's never heard anything. I spent two days searching for her, but I had no luck either. I decided to give up. I get the creeps down here and I was starving. All I get at Finn's is fish and green stuff . . .'

So that was why he looked so fit.

'So I just stopped to search that old chocolate machine. I wrenched it right off the wall, trying to see if I could get the back off it. Then suddenly I heard someone talking to herself. She sounded Scottish, so I thought it could well be Doll. *You'll Never Walk Alone* proves it.'

'Result!' said Elliot. 'Well done, Lewis.'

'It was just a bit of luck,' said Lewis. 'But don't tell anyone yet. I think we should try and get Doll out on our own. I'd like to give Finn a surprise.'

'Come back to ours now and we'll talk it through,' I said. I was actually enjoying his company.

'I'd like to, mate,' said Lewis. 'But I've got to get to the fish market, then back to Finn's. He's clean out of squid.'

'What about tomorrow?' said Elliot.

'I'll be running around all day trying to get hold of systems stuff,' said Lewis, shaking his head. 'I'm helping Finn test his security virus. He's working flat out on it and he needs all the equipment yesterday.'

From the way Lewis talked, he was indispensable to Finn already. They were living in a treehouse on Hampstead Heath. They slept in hammocks, they had one pan to cook in and they survived on supplies that Lewis got on the black market. Finn seemed to be entrusting him with everything. In the end, Lewis agreed to come round on Saturday. Until then, we promised not to tell anyone else about Doll, except Sky.

Lewis gave us the fourth hoverboard.

'This one's for her,' he said. 'It's the newest one and she'll like the design.'

Sky was happy about Doll and really pleased with her hoverboard, which was a Nirvana, and had a silver angel flying through a moonlit sky. But she didn't seem at all pleased that Lewis was coming round on Saturday.

'I have to live with that big lump in our time. Getting away from him was my main reason for coming on this mission. Why did he have to come too? It's a nightmare.'

'I know,' said Elliot sympathetically. 'But think what Finn said about him.'

'If you believe that, you believe anything,' snorted Sky.

'Maybe he has got a good heart,' Elliot said. 'He's found

Doll already, and he's given you the best hoverboard, and he's only getting fishy stuff at Finn's, while we've got the food replicator and Snowy and flume rides and . . .'

'That boring school to go to every day,' I said. 'It's a waste of time. I'd rather be camping out with Finn and getting stuff done.'

'Well, I don't want to meet him,' said Sky. 'Anyway, Marc just rang. He's invited me out for a pizza on Saturday.'

'What?' I said. 'Why do you want to waste time with that old nerd?'

'He's not a nerd,' said Sky. 'He's more of a geek.'

'But you're supposed to be getting matey with Stella Rigg,' I said. 'You're missing the point of the whole operation, swanning around with Marc flipping Marquez.'

'Missing the point am I? Lewis isn't the only one who's had a result. Listen to this.'

She walked up to the phone and said 'Play.'

A 3D image of Stella's face appeared.

'Hello Sky. Thanks for the invite for supper on Friday. But Dad would prefer it if you came here instead. Shame. I'd love to meet your auntie, but Dad's a bit protective. My driver can pick us all up from school and then drop you home later. And please ask Hunter to come – and your little brother as well. We'll have supper and we could mess about in my recording studio. Give me a ring. By-eee.'

She waved and smiled and her image disappeared.

'First objective sorted,' said Sky triumphantly. 'Am I a fast worker or what? I rang back and she was dead pleased

94

when I said you two would come too. I think she likes you, Hunter, but I can't think why.'

She picked up a silver cushion as she spoke and threw it hard at my stomach, then she ran upstairs before I could get her back.

It was a warm evening and Elliot and I sat out on the balcony and played cards. Liz came back and joined us. She was in the short rainbow dress she wears for the weather programme when showers are forecast. She sat down next to us, stretched out her tanned legs and put her feet up on an empty chair. She even had glittering rainbow nail varnish on her toes.

'What's new, pussycat?' she asked Elliot, putting her arm round his shoulders.

'We've seen Lewis and he's found . . .'

I glared at him and shook my head.

'. . . lots of systems stuff for Finn. And we've all got an invitation to the Palace on Friday.'

'Nice work,' said Liz excitedly, jumping up and giving us both a kiss.

Elliot wiped the lipstick off his check with the back of his hand. 'It was Sky who clinched the Palace thing,' he said.

'What a star!' said Liz. 'That is such wonderful news. I'll go and tell Steiner right away.'

After she'd gone, Elliot ordered spaghetti and meatballs for us from the reppy. We ate it out on the balcony looking out at the lights of the city. I thought about the first time we had spaghetti and meatballs, in an Italian restaurant in the old London, after seeing *The Lost World* at the cinema. Elliot must have been quite young, because he got the red sauce all over his white T-shirt. Mum and Dad pretended it was blood and he was a T-Rex. I remember them screaming, 'Something has survived.'

Thinking about Mum and Dad and how much they loved Elliot suddenly got me seriously worried about Rigg and the guards and everything. I realised we couldn't rely on the Jedi hypnosis thing at all. It hadn't worked at the pool, had it? It didn't work when you were frightened and it didn't work without eye contact. I was exposing Elliot to real danger.

But Elliot was enjoying himself. He loved his hoverboard. He loved Snowy, who was sitting next to him gazing up at him with his soft brown eyes and snuffling up any stray bits of meatball. Elliot even liked it at school. He chattered away about it.

'The dance lesson was pants,' he said. 'But the real teacher is OK, and the robot teachers are funky. Plus you don't have to write at all in my class, you just speak into your projector and it displays your words for you.'

'You should try and smuggle yours home with you,' I said.

'I reckon I will,' he said cheerfully.

The only thing he hated was the school reppy. It checked what you had at each meal and it even monitored your diet over the week, telling you if you needed less fat or more dairy foods. Luckily for him, it didn't notice the rude gestures he made and it had no idea what he ate at home. He got a lot of satisfaction from that.

'Warning,' it would say. 'You have made a high fat selection.'

'You should see what I had for breakfast, mate,' he would say, giving it the finger.

They also monitored your physical activity at Regents House. Every time you did sport or dance you showed your ID card to a machine in the hall. If you didn't do enough exercise, you'd get a warning from the network at the end of the week. It also told you off if you did too much.

'It's a police state,' Elliot grumbled. 'Warning. You are breathing too much air. Please take a smaller selection.'

But Elliot was looking forward to representing Regents House in the London schools chess tournament. He actually thought he could win.

'But that's mad,' I blurted out. 'You're only as good as the Total Chess brainfeed, but they'll all have done that. The other kids will be miles better. They'll have worked out some original moves and stuff – gone way beyond the brainfeed.'

Elliot's face fell.

'You're right,' he said, pushing away his plate of spaghetti. 'And people will notice if I don't do well. They might guess I'm not really Elliot McCoy. Why did Mr Slater have to find out about him being a chess champ?'

'And why did Miss Trump agree to enter you?' I said. 'I reckon she might want to expose us. But don't worry, Elliot, we'll probably be gone before the tournament anyway. When is it?'

'Next Monday.'

'Oh,' I said. 'Well, we'll ask Finn's advice. I bet he's brilliant at chess.'

That was enough to reassure Elliot, because he's not

really a worrier. He'd had a good day. He'd made the other kids in his class laugh and he was really pleased about Lewis finding Doll and about our invitation to the palace. He'd even perfected a way of drinking only his favourite layers of CloudNine using precision straw sucking. He chattered on about it all and it made me feel a bit better.

Steiner came the following evening to brief us for the palace.

'Congratulations for getting the invitation, Sky,' he said, shaking her hand enthusiastically. 'We're very impressed. You've achieved your first objective with astonishing speed.

'Now, let me talk you through your visit to the palace. Your objective on Friday is simple: to find an access point to the main security system. Then you can infect it with Finn's virus on a subsequent visit. I've decided to get Wilson to cause a power cut. That will be your chance to have a good look around, without the clones spotting anything on their security cameras. But you'll have to be quick. It won't take them long to switch to other generators. Our source tells us there's an access point in the main green and gold balcony room. The access points are hidden and Rigg moves them around. All we know is that the keys to reveal them are always something Welsh.'

'Something Welsh?' said Sky.

'What like?' said Elliot as Snowy trotted over to sniff Steiner's shoes.

'It could be a harp,' said Steiner vaguely, bending over to stroke Snowy's woolly head. 'Or a daffodil, or indeed a leek . . . anything to do with Wales, that's what our source said.'

was quite lonely. Liz had told her that Stella's mother left home years ago. She was an actress in Hollywood, so Stella didn't see her very much at all.

'Hey Ed,' said Stella as we approached the palace. 'Could you land us on the balcony? Like you did on my birthday last year, when Mum was here?'

'I don't know about that, Stella,' he replied. 'Your father might not like it.'

'Oh please Ed . . . go on.'

'What do you guys reckon?' he asked. 'Do you want to land on the balcony?'

We nodded. It would have been a lot safer to go in through the main door, but we didn't realise that at the time.

As we flew over the massive wrought-iron gates of the palace, we turned in the air and I looked down through the crystal clear glass bubble and saw a golden statue with wings. We hovered in midair, Ed opened the hatch and we climbed down the gleaming silver steps onto a great stone balcony.

'I'll show you my recording studio first,' said Stella.

She led the way through tall French windows into the biggest and most magnificent room I'd ever seen. It was all green and gold and the dazzling chandeliers were reflected in ornate mirrors on every wall.

'This is it,' whispered Sky. 'The main balcony room.'

Somewhere in the room there had to be an access point to the security system. Sky stopped by a bowl of crystal daffodils. She touched them, but nothing happened. The place was stuffed with ornaments and decorations, but we couldn't stop to look around, because Stella hurried through this room into others. As Stella and Sky turned right into a sumptuous red hallway, Elliot went straight on into a blue room to look at a pair of Chinese vases with dragons on top. I followed him.

'Dragons,' he said. 'That's to do with Wales – I've seen it on their rugby strip.'

The dragons had tiny bells on their necks. He touched one of them, but nothing happened. If the little bell rang, we didn't hear it, because the sound was drowned out by a piercing whistle.

We turned to see a man looking at us from the doorway. He was like no one I'd ever seen before. His head was swivelled right round, like an owl's, and he was staring right at us with enormous saucer eyes. His fixed, unblinking gaze made my blood run cold. I looked round for Stella and Sky, but they were nowhere to be seen. Suddenly the man pounded towards us. Before we had time to react, he had grabbed us both round the neck, with an iron grip, and shoved us down on the floor. Then he threw back his head and made the horrible whistling noise again.

I could hear Elliot choking. I tried to look at him, but I couldn't turn my head. The grip on my neck was suffocating. Then I heard the pounding of more powerful feet. Another one had got Sky and he ran across with her and slammed her down on the floor next to us. Then I heard Stella crying out desperately: 'Stop! Please stop! You're making a terrible mistake.'

I thought I was going to pass out, when Stella shouted: 'Daddy! Come and help! Quickly!'

Looming above us was an older, bulkier version of all the clones. He was laughing.

'Please Daddy,' said Stella desperately. 'They're my friends from school. Do something!'

'OK sweetheart, OK,' he said, and he managed to stop laughing long enough to utter one short command. It sounded like 'Cease'.

The iron grip on my neck relaxed and I rolled over on the floor, alongside Elliot and Sky. We sat up, choking and struggling to get our breath back. None of us uttered a word of protest.

'Well, Stella?' said Rigg. 'I should be angry with you for bringing strangers in without security clearance.'

'I'm really sorry, Daddy,' said Stella. 'I thought it would be fun to land on the balcony . . . I forgot all about the new guards . . . I just didn't think.'

'That's OK, honey,' he went on. 'It was a good test for them and it was great to see them in action.'

Rigg held out a large brawny hand to Sky: 'No hard feelings, darling?' he said.

'No sir,' she said, holding out her own trembling hand. Rigg helped Sky to her feet, then stood and watched as Elliot and I struggled to get up. We leaned against the wall and looked at each other.

Just then Rigg's mobile rang. He held it out and it projected a 3D image of two clones holding up an older man. He was in a bad way and could hardly stand.

'Sorry to bother you at home, sir,' said one of the clones. 'But we've got that Mr Rossi, the guy with the restaurants.'

'So I see.'

'He still won't sign. What do you want us to do with him?'

'The usual . . . give him another good kicking if necessary . . . let me know when he has signed . . . don't bother me again till then.'

'Yes sir.'

Rigg pocketed his mobile and the image faded from the air.

'Sorry about that, kids,' said Rigg. 'Just an old trouble-maker. Nothing to worry about.'

Sky raised her eyebrows at me, but said nothing.

'So what do you think of my new guards?' Rigg asked us.

'They're . . . very . . . strong,' said Sky, rubbing her sore neck.

'You bet,' said Rigg. 'They're a damn sight tougher than my clones. Big disappointment some of them. But these new guards are the business. Lovely, aren't they?'

That's not the word I would have chosen. There were three of them in the room now. They weren't identical, but they all had the same powerful build, like Olympic sprinters. They stood, swaying and turning, knees slightly bent, tensed to run or attack in any direction, at an instant. Their heads were rotating continually, like cruel birds of prey, their huge, staring eyes scanning every corner of the room, on constant alert.

Rigg was looking at them with affectionate pride. I'd seen our neighbour look at his pit bull terrier in the same way.

'Come and have a closer look, son,' he said to Elliot. There were livid red marks on Elliot's neck and he was still trembling, but Rigg took no notice. He put a heavy arm round Elliot's thin shoulders and marched him over to the nearest guard. Elliot was sinking under his embrace and I wanted to run over and kick Rigg's fat backside, but of course, I didn't.

'They're androids,' he said. 'And they're virtually indestructible. Feel the power of this one.' He lifted up its arm and pushed back its sleeve. 'Go on, lad.'

Elliot put a reluctant hand on the android's powerful arm. It turned its head to stare at him but did not move.

'They've got a punch like a sledgehammer,' said Rigg. 'You know what they say. Don't hit at all unless you have to, but if you do have to hit, hit hard.'

'But what's to stop them attacking you and Stella?' said Sky.

'The faces of all palace staff and residents are scanned into the androids' central control unit. When they see a face that doesn't match up, they race over and pin 'em down.'

'We noticed,' said Elliot.

Rigg laughed. 'I can also set 'em to stun or kill. Lucky I only chose pin down today, eh kids?' he snorted, slapping poor Elliot hard on the back. Elliot smiled bravely back. He is so great sometimes.

'I'm testing 'em here at the palace, and then I'm going to roll 'em out all over the country. These are lawless times, you know. There's people living rough with no ID. There's even weirdos living in trees! These boys will put a stop to that. Every single person will have to register and have their face scanned in. If there's some that don't want to cooperate, well, I don't fancy their chances much, do you?'

He must have seen the look of horror on Sky's face.

'Don't worry, my lovely,' he said, winking at Sky. 'It's the troublemakers we're after. Not innocent girls like yourself. Your face will be safely scanned in.'

Sky managed a warm smile and Rigg looked at her admiringly.

'I like your new friend,' he said to Stella. 'And her brothers.'

Stella beamed. 'Sky and Hunter are both in my class this year. And Elliot here is a chess champ. He's in a tournament on Monday. You could come and watch.'

'Really?' said Rigg. 'I like chess myself. Maybe I will come along, if I'm not too busy.'

Elliot looked horrified.

'Now, Stell,' he said, turning to his daughter. 'We'd better go down and scan these guys in. That's if you don't want to send 'em home in three wooden boxes!'

We set off back down a long corridor, and as we walked our feet sank into the luxurious blood-red carpet. My heart sank too, as the impossibility of the operation struck home. It was all so gorgeous here at the Palace. Rigg had all the wealth and all the technology on his side. He was untouchable.

Then the lights went out.

'What the blazes?' yelled Rigg.

Wilson had managed to get the power down.

Rigg's mobile rang.

'I'll take this one in private,' he said. 'Take 'em in there a moment, Stell.'

We left him shouting at a clone image in the hallway and went into the room he'd indicated. It was the green and golden room with the balcony.

'Get Stella outside,' Sky whispered to Elliot.

'What's that golden statue with wings, Stella?' said Elliot, taking her hand and leading her out on the balcony.

Now was our chance.

'Try anything,' I whispered. 'Harps, dragons, daffodils, leeks, rugby balls.'

'Tom Jones,' said Sky. 'Hannibal Lecter.'

We raced round the room trying anything and everything. I looked behind a painting of George and the Dragon. I looked for leeks in a tapestry bordered with fruit and vegetables. I tried to find a daffodil on an ornate desk with flower carvings. There was a funny metal statue of Pinocchio on top of the desk. His long nose had a razor sharp tip and I tested it with my finger. Suddenly the roll-top desk lid rattled open and a console appeared.

Bingo! But why?

Sky looked round in alarm. 'Shut it up quickly,' she said.

I touched Pinocchio again and the desk lid rattled back up.

Rigg stuck his big head round the door.

'Come on Stell,' he shouted. 'We're going down to the control room.'

As we walked down the grand staircase, all the lights came back on.

'About time,' said Rigg.

He opened a heavy metal door and showed us into a brightly lit room full of screens and controls. It was manned by a clone and there were two androids scanning the wall of screens, which showed what was going on in every corner of the palace. They turned their huge eyes on us as soon as we entered and flexed ready to spring.

My blood ran cold and I heard Elliot's sharp intake of breath behind me.

'Cease,' said Rigg again, grinning with pleasure as the androids obeyed him and relaxed.

Then he turned to the clone.

'Power's up again then, Nelson?'

'Yes, sir.'

'I want a full report on my desk tomorrow morning. I am making you personally responsible for ensuring that it cannot happen again.'

'Yes, sir.'

Rigg turned to Stella.

'How long are your friends staying?' he asked.

'Well,' she said. 'We're going to do some recording and have some supper. It is Friday, after all, Daddy.'

'Scan 'em in until nine thirty, Nelson,' said Rigg to the clone. 'Daddy's got work to do now, sweetheart,' he said, giving Stella a kiss on the cheek. 'Make sure you're out of here before half nine,' he said to us. 'That's if you want to go home in one piece.' With that he winked at Sky, thumped Elliot and me on the shoulder and left the room.

The clone, Nelson, told us to stand in front of a large

screen on the wall. It came to life and we saw a reflection of our faces in it.

'Request security clearance,' he said. 'Start time – now. End time – 9.30. That's it. You're safe now. But please get them out of here in good time, Stella, remember what happened to that carpenter. We don't want another scandal.'

'What did happen to the carpenter, Stella?' said Elliot.

'Oh, nothing too bad,' said Stella, looking shifty. 'He's getting the best possible care and his condition is stable, I think, isn't it Nelson?'

Nelson shook his head and made a throat-cutting gesture.

'Oh dear,' said Stella, looking momentarily dismayed. 'And it was all my fault in a way. He was working outside on the windows . . . and I just asked him to step inside for a minute to see if he could fix my jewellery box.' Her lip trembled. I thought she was going to cry for a second, but then her face brightened up. 'Never mind,' she said. 'He was only a carpenter and I didn't do it on purpose. I can't be expected to remember everything.'

I thought about my dad's friend Martin, who is also a carpenter.

'Now come and see my recording studio,' said Stella. 'It's brand new.'

The studio was on the top floor next to Stella's private rooms. We passed a couple of androids on the way. I froze, but the system worked and they let us walk past unmolested.

You wouldn't think we could relax at all after that. But we actually had a great time in the recording studio, because it was serious fun. You just hummed in a tune and it played it back to you, with drums, bass, backing vocals, anything you fancied. Then you could put it all together in a 3D video, choosing from this great library of images and filming yourself in amongst them.

I'm not much of a singer, so I was the director and I really enjoyed myself. Stella wanted to do a version of this song 'Storm on Love Island' that was a big hit. So I chose an image of a black volcanic island and made big waves crash on the beach. I got the others to sing and dance on the black sand amongst this chorus line of surfers and mermaids. Sky has a good voice and Elliot is a great dancer. Stella was OK too – and she had a great time.

'Put some sea-creatures in, Hunter,' she said. 'Ooh look guys, look at the funny crabs, look at them dance.'

I fiddled around with the sound to add more depth to Stella's voice and fiddled around with the video to make her hair shinier and her eyes brighter. She was thrilled with the result.

'This is so fab,' she kept saying. 'I'm so glad you guys could come round.'

As you can imagine, however, we kept a close eye on the time. None of us wanted to end up in a stable condition in some secret palace clinic. We had supper out on the balcony of her private sitting room, looking out on the palace gardens and the lake. A pigeon landed on the stone balustrade. Elliot was going to feed it some of his pizza, but Stella slapped the bird away.

'Daddy says they're vermin,' she said. 'We mustn't encourage them.'

We left at nine o'clock sharp.

When we got back to the flat, we got ourselves a Sparx each, then decided on a game of pool to calm ourselves down. It was Elliot and Sky against me.

'He was only a carpenter,' said Elliot in a squeaky-voiced imitation of Stella Rigg.

'What is she like?' I said. 'Dad's friend Martin is a carpenter.'

'So was Jesus,' said Sky, as she chalked up her cue.

'They've got no respect for human life,' I said, breaking hard and making a red ball jump right off the table. 'None at all.'

'What did you think of Rigg?' said Sky.

'I think he should spell his name with a P,' said Elliot.

'Well, at least you found the access point, Hunter,' said Sky, neatly potting a yellow, then another yellow.

'I'm not so sure it was,' I said. 'Why would Pinocchio be the key?'

Sky shook her head.

'I get it,' said Elliot triumphantly, potting another yellow. 'It's obvious.'

'Tell us,' said Sky.

'Work it out for yourselves,' said Elliot.

'Tell us,' said Sky. And she started to tickle him.

'He went inside one, didn't he,' said Elliot, giggling.

'Went inside what?'

'A whale. Steiner thought it was Wales, but he got it wrong, it was whales.'

Brilliant. So it was the access point to the security system.

'But those androids?' Sky said. 'I wasn't expecting anything like that.'

'Neither was I,' I said, and I suddenly felt very angry. 'Why the hell didn't Steiner warn us about them?' I shouted, potting the black by mistake and losing the game.

'I bet he didn't even know about them,' said Elliot.

'In that case, I think we should call the whole thing off,' I said, throwing down my cue. 'And next time they pick us for a mission to the future, remind me to say no.'

Eureka! In the bath later on, I had a brilliant idea. Why hadn't I thought of it before? We didn't need to put our lives at risk at the Palace. We had the time machine. We could go back in time to before Rigg was born and get rid of his mother – like the Terminator. I rang Steiner and asked him to come round right away.

I got Steiner a semi-skimmed decaff cappuccino and we sat down on the big sofa together. But Steiner wasn't keen on my plan at all.

'Absolutely out of the question,' he said, sounding outraged. 'What about the sanctity of human life? We have no quarrel with Rigg's mother. And what about Stella? If we got rid of Rigg, she wouldn't be here. Neither would the clones – and some of them are quite good men apparently. Thousands of lives would be affected – maybe even mine.'

'Well,' I said, thinking hard. 'Of course we wouldn't kill Rigg's mother or anything . . . we could just send her and the baby Rigg off to another time.'

'You forgot the chocolate,' said Steiner and he went over

to the reppy, put his cup of coffee back in and asked it to dust the foam with plain chocolate and give him a bourbon biscuit.

'No,' he said sternly. 'The whole thing could have unimaginable consequences. We will stick to plan A.'

'But what about the androids?' I shouted. 'They're deadly. You didn't warn us about them. I don't think you even knew about them.'

'I confess that I was not aware that they were operational yet,' he said, avoiding my eye. 'It's a great pity Doll's not around to help us. There's nothing she doesn't know about artificial intelligence. But you're not to worry about those androids,' he said, draining his coffee and making for the door. 'I'm sure that Finn and Wilson can bodge up some way of scanning your faces in.'

And that was really reassuring, wasn't it?

11
An Old Friend

I woke early on Saturday morning. My dreams had been haunted by Finn's words:

I see danger for Elliot . . . watch out for owl eyes.

It didn't seem so mad any more.

I went into Elliot's room but he was still fast asleep. He looks small when he's sleeping, because he curls up, and in his golden pyjamas he looked like a little hamster. We were going back to Rigg's palace as soon as Sky managed to get another invitation. What if something happened to Elliot? How would Mum ever get over it?

He stirred, looked at me crossly and squinted at his watch.

'Why are you waking me now?' he groaned. 'It's only just gone six, you wally.'

That cheered me up a bit.

'It's Saturday,' I said. 'Lewis is coming round later to talk about Doll. I just thought . . . I'd go for a swim before breakfast.'

As I said it I decided to do just that. The exercise would destress me and give me a chance to unravel my thoughts. They taught you that at school in Relaxation.

I only felt a small twinge of fear as I launched myself off into the flume. This time it was *The Great Escape* music playing and I hummed along as I swung round the curves and shot down the straights. I lay down, enjoying the rush of water round my head and by the time I flew through the air at the end – and sank deep down into the blue water in a crowd of tiny bubbles – I couldn't even remember what I was worried about.

There was nobody else down there. I started doing lengths, enjoying the feel of my strong crawl strokes pulling me silently through the water like a shark. I was Sharkman, bitten by a radioactive hammerhead as a small child and with a mission to stamp out crime at sea.

I dived underwater. I was 007, racing to free the beautiful Chinese girl chained to the hull of the enemy's ship.

I surfaced, and then spun round in shock as I realised that the echoing silence had been broken by a splash behind me. Which flume had it come from?

Someone was swimming underwater towards me. I panicked and plunged off towards the side with the steps. But strong hands grabbed my ankles and dragged me back. I went under and came up spluttering. I turned round and saw a man with white-blond hair and heavy dark stubble. His pale blue eyes looked at me with great interest.

'Yo Hunter!' he said. 'Your swimming's improved.'

I looked at him in amazement.

'Don't you recognise me?' he said. 'We've met twice before you know.'

I knew who it was all right, but where was his moustache and his black hair?

'I'll give you a clue,' he went on. 'The first time we met, you shot me and the second time we met, you dive-bombed my colleague, Alex. Now do you know who I am?'

'You're Stan,' I said. 'And I'm sorry I shot you.'

He put his hands on my shoulders and looked at me closely.

'Brown eyes,' he said thoughtfully. 'Very unusual. I wonder where you come from, Hunter?'

I didn't like wearing the green contact lenses in the water. And stupidly, I'd forgotten to put on my goggles. I was shaking with fear, but I tried to sound confident:

'What do you want?' I squeaked.

'I want to ask you a few questions,' he explained. 'Quick . . . before anyone else comes.'

He grabbed my arm and frogmarched me out of the water and over to a narrow door that I'd never really noticed before. It was an old, disused sauna room, full of cleaning stuff and folding chairs. There was a wide wooden bench and a large leather bag on the floor. He threw me a towel and told me to sit down on the bench. He wrapped himself in another and sat down on one of the chairs. As he did so he caught sight of himself in the large mirror on the wall.

He frowned at his reflection, gave a long sigh and reached for the bag. He took out a knife, with a long, wicked blade. I watched in horror as he pulled a long blond hair out of his head and held it up. He slashed at it with the knife and the lower half fell soundlessly to the floor.

'Nice and sharp,' he said.

I gave a moan of fear.

'I wish I didn't have to do this . . .' he said, turning to face me.

Desperately I tried the Jedi hypnosis thing, but I couldn't focus. I was too scared. I looked around for a weapon instead. I grabbed a broom, jumped to my feet, picked it up and held it like a staff, hoping to block his attack.

'But there's no other way,' he continued, looking back at his reflection. 'This dark stubble is a real giveaway and you can't keep dyeing it.'

Then he got a tube out of his bag, plastered cream on his face and started to scrape away at the stubble with the razor-sharp blade.

I laughed then and he looked at me strangely.

'You're easily amused,' he said.

'I thought you were going to use the knife on me,' I explained, putting back the broom and sitting down again.

He looked hurt.

'Why does everyone think that we clones are all the same? I'd never do a thing like that. It's against everything Mrs Rossi ever taught me.'

'Mrs Rossi?'

'She looked after me at nursery. I was very fond of her. That's one reason why I've left the guards. Rigg's taken over Mr Rossi's restaurants. He's saying Mr Rossi didn't pay his taxes. It's a disgrace. I know Rigg is my father in a sense, but I don't want any more to do with him. So I'm very grateful to you, Hunter.'

'Grateful?'

'You bet. Jumping on Alex like that at the pool . . . gave me the boot up the backside I needed. I knew I'd get into trouble for letting you get away with it, so I had to do a runner. You forced me into it and I'm much obliged. Thank you.'

'You're welcome,' I said politely.

'He nearly drowned, you know.'

'Nearly?'

Stan nodded.

What a relief!

'He's fine now. I don't know what to do with him. I've locked him up in my spare bedroom, with a reppy and an entertainment device, but he can't stay there for ever. I've never liked the guy. And he's even worse in a confined space.

'Anyway,' he went on. 'I had to come and see you. The way you and your brother stood up to Alex. I've never seen anything like it. No regular young people are capable of that and you don't look quite like other young people either. Your body language, your anger . . . it's more like us clones. And then there's your eye colour.'

He put one hand on my shoulder and looked straight into my eyes.

'I want to know who you are and what you're up to, Hunter. Maybe I could help?'

I said nothing. I couldn't help liking Stan. And he could be a major help to us at the palace. But would it be right to trust him? Or was he a spy sent by Rigg?

I decided to try the Jedi thing one more time. I took a deep breath, focused hard on Stan and did a little test.

'Pick up the broom, Stan.'

A look of total relaxation came over Stan's face and he walked over to the broom and picked it up.

'Sweep the floor.'

And he began to sweep all the dust on the floor into one corner. He did a really thorough job.

'How come you're so good at cleaning?'

'Used to have to keep the barracks spotless.'

'Why are you in disguise?'

'I'm a deserter. I'm in hiding.'

'Why did you come back to see me?'

'I liked you,' he said. 'And your little brother. You were both so scared and yet so courageous. I wanted to find out what you were up to. You were lucky with Alex. But you don't know how vicious some of us clones can be. I wanted to warn you . . . maybe even to help you.'

'What do you think of Rigg?' I asked. 'Do you think he should stay as president?'

'No I don't. He's made this a bad country.'

'Would you help us get Rigg out?'

There was a long pause.

'Yes I would.'

I did the triple blink to release him from the hypnosis. He returned to the mood he'd been in before, gave me a searching look and repeated his last question.

'I want to know who you are and want you're up to, Hunter.'

'I'd like to tell you,' I said truthfully, 'but I can't until I've cleared it with the others.'

'Others?' he said. 'So that pretty girl's involved . . . and Liz McCoy, the weather girl?'

I said nothing.

'You're going to Stella Rigg's school, aren't you?'

I nodded.

'Are you trying to get Rigg out?'

'I can't say.'

'OK,' he said. 'But remember, I've worked at the Palace. I know the guys there. They're not all as bad as they look. Promise you'll be in touch if you need me. Here's my number. Ask for Mr Bulstani. Just say . . . you need some advice on gardening . . . and I'll know it's you.'

As I went back up in the lift, I was very grateful that I hadn't had a real gun back in Finn's treehouse. If I had, I might have killed Stan. He seemed like the enemy then, but now I saw that he was probably our best hope. If we could trust him, we were in with a chance at the palace after all. I had to talk to Steiner about it as soon as possible. I suddenly wanted to get the whole thing done and dusted. Then I could take Elliot safely back home.

I had my chance to tell Steiner when he came round later that morning, when Sky and Elliot had gone for a swim. Unfortunately, Miss Trump was with him. She'd brought some more maths brainfeeds for us. She said we still weren't up to scratch and the teachers had noticed, but I couldn't help feeling she had come to spy on us.

I got them each a cappuccino. I even remembered to get the foam dusted with chocolate and got a bourbon biscuit placed on each saucer.

'I've got something to tell you,' I said. 'I've just been talking to the clone, Stan.'

Steiner's coffee washed over into the saucer as he crashed the cup down onto the table.

'Did he come to find you again?' said Steiner.

'Yes, sir.' I'd noticed that he liked it when I called him that. It was the kind of thing we discussed in Verbal Skills.

'Is he going to report us?'

'No, sir. He said he could help us. He knows the Palace, you see, and the clones who work there. He says they're not all as bad as they look.'

'All those young men are exact genetic replicas of the President – and we know how evil he is.'

'But when I said Lewis was evil you said it was ridiculous. And you were right . . . I see that now.'

'Lewis is one thing. A clone is quite another,' said Steiner, avoiding my eye.

'But when you vetoed my Terminator plan you said some of the clones were good men.'

I had him there.

Miss Trump got herself a Tranquilade and gulped it straight down.

'Are you saying you've revealed the details of our plans to a Rigg clone?' she said.

'I haven't. But I'd like to. I know I can trust him, you see,' I blurted out. 'I checked him out under Jedi hypnosis.'

Steiner gave a contemptuous snort.

'Get real, Hunter,' he said. 'If Stan approaches you again, deny everything. You won the lottery . . . you moved to London . . . that is all.'

'OK, sir,' I said, but I didn't mean it. From what I'd

seen of the Palace, I knew it was too risky without Stan, and I wasn't prepared to put Elliot in any more danger.

'So you think Stan's all right but Steiner won't believe it?' said Elliot later, tearing up a ring doughnut. He gave half to an ecstatic Snowy and munched the other half himself.

'Yeah,' I said gloomily. 'He got really rattled.'

'Well, I think Stan sounds brilliant,' Sky said. 'We need a bit of inside help at the Palace. Steiner and Wilson haven't seen those androids in action.'

'I know,' I groaned. 'Perhaps you could talk to Steiner. You're brilliant in Verbal Skills. He might listen to you.'

Sky got her Post-it notes out. There was one of her lists on the top sheet:

1. Wash hair
2. Look up Grand National winners?
3. Ask reppy for crepes suzettes

She screwed it up and started another one:

1. Persuade Steiner to accept Stan
2. Sort out androids
3. Free Doll

'I've got a brilliant idea,' said Sky, finally. 'We'll ask Stan to help us get Doll out. He might even know the prison guards. If that works, Steiner will have to trust him, won't he? Then we'll have Stan and Doll in our corner against the androids.'

'That is brilliant,' said Elliot.

'We'll tell Lewis today,' I said.

'Lewis,' groaned Sky. 'I'd forgotten about him.'

Elliot laughed.

'Lewis is all right, Sky.'

'That's easy for you to say. You don't have to live with him. You don't have to listen to him bleeping his Game-Boy and slurping and chomping his food . . . every single day of your life.'

'I tell you what,' I said. 'Ignore him as much as you like back home, just try and get on with him here.'

'Pretend this Lewis is a different person,' said Elliot. 'OK?'

'OK.'

The funny thing was, Lewis did seem to be a different person. Either that, or I was. Sky cancelled her pizza with Marc and when Lewis arrived, she kept her word. She got him a burger and some lightning chips from the reppy and Elliot got him a bottle of CloudNine. Maybe he did slurp a bit. But nobody's perfect, are they?

Snowy seemed to like him all right. He came and sat at his feet and looked longingly up at his chips. While Lewis ate we told him about Stan. He saw the possibilities straight away.

'Excellent,' he said, as he gave the last bit of burger to a grateful Snowy. 'That Stan is just what we need. I bet he will know how to break into Doll's prison. He probably even knows the prison guards.'

'Why don't you call him now, Hunter?' said Sky.

I got out my mobile and asked it for Mr Bulstani.

The dialling tone went on and on and I was about to give up when a man answered.

'Hello?' he said, but his voice was muffled and I couldn't make the image of his face appear.

'Hello,' I said. 'Can I speak to Mr Bulstani?'

'Yo, dude,' said Stan.

'Er . . . yo,' I replied. 'It's me . . . I need your advice about gardening . . . there's this plant we want to move.'

'No worries,' he said. 'I'll be round in half an hour. I'll bring my spade.'

12
Springing Doll

Stan was round in ten minutes. He was wearing white shorts and silver jewellery and his blond hair was in a ponytail. You would never have guessed he was a Rigg clone; he looked more like a surfer than a guard.

'Four of you?' he said. 'Cool.'

I introduced him to the others and he sat down next to Sky on the sofa.

'So you want to move a plant?'

Sky smiled.

'It's this person called Doll,' she said. 'Lewis here found out where she is and we want to rescue her.'

'You wanna spring Doll? The GM Genius? That is not gonna be easy. She's Rigg's secret weapon.'

'Secret weapon?'

'You bet. She's into all this crazy thought control stuff. There's a couple of clones in deep trouble for making an illegal brainfeed based on her hypnosis work.'

Elliot nudged me.

'But it's her work on memory erasure that's got Rigg excited,' said Stan. 'Rigg gets away with murder, but he'd rather release the people he's done over. If he could wipe their memory of what happened, he could even keep them on his side.'

'I don't think she'd help him with that,' said Sky.

'That's why he's locked her up then. Rigg is not the most patient guy in the world; I reckon Doll's in danger.'

'We've got to get her out as soon as possible,' said Sky.

'Too right,' said Elliot. 'Steiner said she'd know how to fix the androids and we need all the help we can get with them.'

'Anyway, I promised I'd find her,' said Lewis. 'Finn really misses her and there's only two like them.'

'Lucky them,' sighed Stan. 'They measured their brains, you know. They say they're bigger than normal people's.'

'I can believe it,' said Elliot. 'No ordinary brain could have invented time travel like Finn did.' He clapped his hand on his mouth, but the cat was out of the bag.

Stan whistled.

'So that's where you guys are coming from?' he said. Then he looked round at each of us in turn and grinned. 'That explains a lot. When are you from?'

'The beginning of the century,' said Sky.

Stan looked delighted. 'Wow,' he said. 'Have you ever been in a motor car?'

We all nodded.

'Wow!' he said. 'Doesn't it smell terrible? With all that smoke coming out of that tube at the back. And aren't people getting run over all over the place?'

'Not so that you'd notice,' I said.

'The turn of the century!' said Stan. 'That is so weird.

Do you know any drug addicts and alcoholics? And psychos, do you know any psychos?'

'Not unless you count these three,' said Sky. 'I think you may have an exaggerated view.'

Stan was shaking his head in wonder.

'Do you place ice hockey and football and all those violent games?'

'We play football,' said Elliot. 'But it's not what you'd call violent.'

'Unless you're playing with Lewis,' I said, and then wished I hadn't.

But Lewis didn't seem to have noticed. He was obviously thinking about Doll.

'Have you still got that other can of Irn-Bru, Elliot?' he said.

We came up with a pretty smart plan for rescuing Doll and we decided to put it into action the very next morning. Then we celebrated with a treat from the reppy. Sky asked it for five crepes suzettes. They turned out to be sweet pancakes on fire with blue flames, like a Christmas pudding.

'My granny makes these,' said Lewis.

'I know,' said Sky. 'That's why I wanted to try them, because she said she'd make them for us on bonfire night . . . I like your granny.'

'Yeah,' said Lewis. 'And she likes you.'

Next morning, Stan swung into action. He waylaid one of Doll's guards as he made his way to his prison shift. He shot a sedative into his arm, using Elliot's stun gun. Then he took him back home and locked him up with Alex, the clone from the swimming pool. Poor Stan. It was getting pretty crowded in his flat, but he couldn't let them go or they'd report him.

Then Stan dyed his hair black again, changed into the guard's prison uniform and shades and went to the prison. He was armed only with an inflatable dolphin that we'd pinched from the sauna room at Bickenhall Mansions. It was folded up in his pocket.

Meanwhile, the three of us set off to meet Lewis down by the old chocolate machine at eight o'clock. Snowy ran along happily beside our hoverboards.

'I really don't think you should bring Snowy, Elliot,' said Sky. 'Nip back and take him home. He might not like it underground.'

'He'll be fine,' said Elliot. 'I'll pick him up when we get down there. Wilson said we should take him out with us whenever we can. He needs the exercise.'

'Not every single day?'

'Yes, every single day,' said Elliot stubbornly. 'He's stuck in all day when we're at school so he has to come with us at weekends.'

Sky gave up. You can't argue with Elliot when he's made up his mind about something.

We had no trouble finding the old warehouse again and it was fun zooming down the abandoned tube lines to meet Lewis. Sky beat us by a whisker, because she had the best hoverboard.

Lewis grinned and put a finger to his lips as we arrived.

'Listen out for the signal,' he whispered, as he lifted the chocolate machine carefully off its brackets.

The signal was supposed to be Stan switching on his radio. Instead, we heard a loud explosion and a rumble of falling bricks. Snowy yelped and jumped back up into Elliot's arms.

'Sounds like Stan nicked some of my bangers,' said Elliot, who had great faith in his firecrackers.

'What is he up to?' said Sky.

'It came from way off that way,' said Lewis, pointing down the tube tunnel. 'Nothing to do with Stan.'

Then we heard Stan's radio blasting out. That was my signal. It meant that Stan had got into Doll's cell and was looking for the other entrance to the ventilation shaft. Covered by the sound of the radio, I used the laser tool that Stan had given me to cut all around the airbrick. A square tunnel appeared.

We all had a good look down it. At first there was only darkness, then we could see a square of light. Stan and Doll must have unblocked the shaft at the other end. We waited. We heard shuffling and eventually a face appeared. We couldn't see her very well in the dim light, but we could see that she was smiling, just like her brother. We reached up to help her down.

As we took her weight, I stumbled backwards and twisted my ankle.

'Are you all right, son?' she asked, kindly.

'Yes,' I lied.

She beamed round at us.

'Your nice friend Stan says you've come to take me to Finn. He says you're trying to topple Rigg. I don't know who you are, but I'm so grateful to you,' she said. 'I don't think I could have taken another day cooped up with those idiotic clones.'

'We'll tell you who we are later,' said Sky. 'I think we should get out of here first.'

Nobody had thought to get another hoverboard for Doll, so she shared Sky's and we shot off down the abandoned tube line towards Finn's secret hideout. My ankle was killing me and I stopped to look at the swelling.

'Keep up, Hunter!' shouted Lewis. 'We can't afford to wait for you.'

He was right, I suppose. I swallowed my annoyance and sped after them.

Suddenly they all swerved to a halt. In front of us was an enormous mound of rubble that completely blocked the tunnel.

'So that's what that explosion was,' said Sky.

'What now?' said Elliot.

'We'll have to turn back,' said Lewis. 'I'm sorry, Doll. We won't be able to go straight to Finn's hideout. We'll have to go back into town.'

I was disappointed. I'd been looking forward to seeing Finn's new treehouse and the look on his face when he saw his sister.

We stopped at the foot of the old iron staircase.

'Won't it be dangerous?' I said. 'Taking Doll out in the open?'

Lewis shrugged.

'What else can we do?' he said.

Lewis turned up our hoverboard lights and we all looked at Doll. She was pretty noticeable. Like Finn, she had greyish skin and a permanent smile on her face. What's more, she was dressed in a pair of striped pyjamas.

'What do you expect if you come barging in on a Sunday morning?' she said.

'Actually, I thought you might need some sort of disguise,' said Sky. 'So I brought this.'

She took off her backpack and pulled out a pair of wraparound shades, an umbrella and the pink hooded sweatshirt she wore for basketball.

Doll squeezed into the pink sweatshirt and pulled the hood tight round her face. It was long and baggy on Sky, but it was tight on Doll and short, revealing all of her striped pyjamas trousers. The sleeves were short too, revealing quite a lot of grey arm. She put the shades on next and turned to look at Elliot and me.

The effect was quite sinister and I had to stifle a scream.

'What do you reckon?' she said.

'I reckon it better be raining,' said Elliot. 'Then you can hide under the brolly.'

It would have to do. Doll took a look up the spiralling iron stairs.

'That is going to be a long hard climb,' she said.

'Have a swig of this,' said Lewis, taking the can out of his pack.

Doll gave a cry of delight.

'Lovely, orangey Irn-Bru,' she said. 'Where on earth did you get it?'

We said nothing. Then she examined the sell-by date on the top of the can and laughed.

'I thought there was something different about you

lot. Finn's made a breakthrough in his time stuff, hasn't he?'

We nodded.

Doll sat down on the steps, tore open the can and took a swig with great pleasure, gazing at us thoughtfully all the while with her kind black eyes. We sat down on the platform and watched her.

'You know that pirate brainfeed on hypnosis?' I asked her. 'Is it true that it's based on your work?'

'That phony Jedi thing? One of my guards produced it. But nobody can get it to work, thank goodness.'

'We can,' said Elliot.

'You can? Fascinating! None of the clones managed it. Maybe you've mastered it because you're still young.'

'But we can't do it when we're nervous,' I said.

'Interesting,' she said. 'Sounds like your relaxation skills aren't up to it.'

'Is it true that you know how to wipe out people's memories?' said Sky.

Doll's permanent smile faded a little.

'I terminated that research,' she said sharply. 'It was meant to help people cope with trauma . . . but it's open to abuse.'

'But could you make it work? If it was for a really good reason?'

'Such as?'

Sky explained how Stan was stuck with two clones: Alex and now the prison guard.

'They'll drive him crazy,' said Sky. 'But he can't let them go or they'll report him.'

'I'd do anything for that lovely Stan,' said Doll. 'I'd wipe the memories of everyone in London.'

'And will you be able to help Finn fix the androids?' I said.

'The new androids at the Palace?' said Doll, shaking the last few drops of Irn-Bru out onto her tongue. 'I'd heard rumours about them, but I didn't know they were up and running already. Don't worry. I'll get them sorted. There's nothing I don't know about artificial intelligence.'

Lewis was on his feet, getting agitated.

'We really should get going,' he said.

'You're right,' said Doll, crumpling up her can. 'Tea time's over.'

'I'll do a reccy up the stairs,' said Lewis. 'Wait there.'

He crept up the spiral stairs, keeping flat against the wall like a secret agent. What a prat! A couple of weeks living rough with Finn, and now he thought he was in the SAS. We waited for what seemed like ages and then he reappeared.

'The coast is clear,' he said, dramatically. 'Follow me in silence . . . and make sure you keep up this time, Hunter.'

He still knew how to really get on my nerves.

We picked up the hoverboards and hurried up the staircase behind him. I did my best to ignore the pain in my ankle.

Lewis reached the top of the stairs first, but he took a sharp intake of breath and crouched back down.

'There's someone there,' he said.

'Let me see,' whispered Sky, clambering past him and peering over the top of the wooden crate.

'There's two clones,' she said. 'And someone else. That's funny. It looks a bit like Miss Trump.'

I took a look. There were three people silhouetted in the open doorway of the warehouse. The shorter, stouter figure wore a suit. It could have been Miss Trump. It could even have been Wilson. Whoever it was, it gestured urgently in our direction, then hurried off. The clones walked purposefully towards the wooden crate.

'Could you hypnotise them, Hunter?' said Sky.

I shook my head.

'Can't make eye contact,' I said.

'Can't relax,' said Elliot.

Instead I took careful aim at one of them. Sky did the same.

'Better wait till they're closer,' I said and we watched them walking steadily towards us. One was wearing cowboy boots, which clicked as he walked across the concrete floor. The other had a completely shaven head. A shaft of dusty light came from the single skylight in the roof. We could see their faces clearly.

'Now,' said Sky.

Two shots rang out and both men fell.

'Peg it,' said Elliot.

We clambered out of the wooden crate, jumped on the hovers and zoomed for the doorway. The alleyway was empty, but I suddenly realised that Lewis wasn't with us. I looked back and saw him limping across the warehouse examining his hoverboard anxiously.

Typical, I thought. You think you're so hard and then you go and hurt yourself at the vital moment. Resisting the urge to leave him there, I hovered over and helped him check his board. There were spider's webs in the turbo air vent. I blew them out and shook it and got it working again.

'Thanks mate,' said Lewis, grinning at me apologetically.

'You're welcome,' I said and punched him in the arm.

The alleyway was still empty and we were almost away when Snowy suddenly jumped from Elliot's arms and ran back to sniff and bark at the two clones. Before I knew it, Elliot had gone running back to get him.

The clone in cowboy boots was sitting up. The anesthetic couldn't have taken a proper hold.

'Get Doll out of here,' I said to Lewis. 'We'll take care of the clones.'

Lewis hesitated for a moment, then shot off with Doll on his hoverboard. 'I'll take her to Finn's another way,' he yelled. 'Good luck.'

To our horror, the clone reached out and grabbed Elliot. Snowy was circling them, snarling and snapping at the cowboy boots. I whipped out my stun gun, but the trigger button jammed.

I was quietly cursing Finn when there was a sudden volley of small explosions and the clone threw himself to the ground. Elliot grabbed his hover and zoomed over to join Snowy behind the crate.

'I knew those bangers would come in handy,' he shouted.

The clone ran after him, but Sky took aim and fired. The dart struck his shoulder, but bounced off harmlessly onto the floor. He turned to face us and reached for his holster.

'Dart-proof clothes!' yelled Elliot from behind the crate. 'Aim for his head.'

Another shot rang out and the clone fell to the floor with a thump.

She had got him in the neck.

'Beautiful shot, Sky,' I said.

'Come on, Snowy,' said Elliot, running out to join us. 'Let's get out before the other one wakes up.'

When we got back to the flat, it was empty. We were all very worried and didn't know what to do. We went out on the balcony and got a drink.

'Do you think Lewis got away all right?' said Sky.

'No question,' said Elliot, slurping up his coke through a straw. 'He's a pretty cool guy. But was that really Miss Trump you saw talking to those two clones, Sky?'

'It could have been,' she said.

'You couldn't tell,' I said. 'It was just a short, fat silhouette in the doorway.'

'Whoever it was, I don't like the way those clones were expecting us,' said Sky.

'But nobody could have tipped them off,' said Elliot. 'The only other person who knew about the Doll thing was Stan.'

'I hope Stan's all right,' said Sky.

'I'm sure he's fine,' I said, as I thumped my stun gun mobile on the tiled floor. I'd discovered that if I slammed it down hard enough, the trigger handle clicked out, even though the button was jammed.

Suddenly it rang.

'You took care of them all right then?' said Lewis.

'In the end.'

'Well done, mate. Top job. I've got someone on the line for you.'

I switched to speaker mode so the others could hear.

'I want to thank you, my friends,' said Finn's voice. 'From the bottom of my heart. You and Lewis and Mr Bulstani have done a marvellous deed today. The best thing that's happened round here for years.'

We all beamed with pride.

'I must go now. I shouldn't really have called. You will never know how much it means to me and my sister to be reunited. Thank you.'

The connection went dead. I stuck my mobile back in my holster but it rang again. Elliot snatched it out and answered it.

'Yo, dude,' said the speaker.

'Stan the man!' said Elliot. 'How did it go?'

'It went like a dream. But this flat is a nightmare. They're both locked up in the spare room with a reppy watching loud films and eating these really smelly kebabs. I don't think I can take much more of it.'

'We've asked Doll to sort it out.'

'Tell her it's an emergency. I don't want blood on my hands.'

'She'll be in touch as soon as she can. Goodbye, Stan.'

'*Hasta la vista*, timelord.'

Stan told us later that he got past the guards with no problem at all. Doll turned up her radio loud and they found the entrance to the ventilation shaft by pulling Doll's sink off the wall. The sound must have travelled up the overflow. He helped Doll into the shaft and fixed the sink back as best he could. Then he inflated the blow-up dolphin and put it in Doll's bed under the blanket. He left the prison asking another guard to cover for him, as he didn't feel well.

'I thought you weren't looking yourself, mate,' said the other guard, kindly. 'You go home and put your feet up.'

Later on that evening we had a surprise visit from Steiner.

'I've just heard the wonderful news about Doll,' he said, shaking all our hands enthusiastically. 'You and Lewis have been truly heroic. Could I trouble you for a cup of tea?'

'Don't forget Stan,' I said, getting him a mug of tea with lemon and a plate of bourbon biscuits. 'We couldn't have done it without him.'

'Yes indeed, I can see that Stan's contribution was crucial,' said Steiner, looking down at the tray. 'Lovely tea, Hunter, but I do prefer it in a proper teacup. Would you mind? And ask for some rich tea biscuits please, I only eat the bourbons with coffee.'

'Did you hear about our problems down in the tube?' said Sky, as I went back to the reppy. 'An explosion blocked off one exit and there were two clones at the other one.'

'And the one in cowboy boots kicked you, didn't he Snowy?' said Elliot, scowling at the memory and feeding Snowy one of the rejected bourbon biscuits.

'They seemed to be expecting us,' said Sky. 'They were

even wearing dart-proof clothes. Somebody must have tipped them off. There was another older, stouter person there with them. We thought it looked a bit like Miss Trump, or maybe even Wilson.'

'Make your mind up,' said Steiner, dunking a rich tea into his cup. 'Couldn't you even tell what gender it was?'

'It was only a silhouette in a doorway,' I said.

'It could have been anyone,' said Steiner. 'Except those two. As I've told you before, my team is one hundred percent loyal. Did they know about your plan to release Doll?'

'No,' I admitted.

'There you are then. It couldn't have been them. All the same, it is extremely worrying to think that those clones might have been lying in wait for you. There are clones crawling all over London at the moment. So be very careful from now on,' he said, making for the door. 'Discretion is the better part of valour, remember.'

13
Checkmate

As soon as I woke up next morning, I remembered that it was the day of Elliot's chess tournament – and we'd forgotten to ask Finn for advice.

'Help!' I said, running into Elliot's room. 'It's that chess thing. What are we going to do?'

Elliot was sitting up in bed eating a sausage sandwich he'd got from the reppy. Poking out from the bottom of the duvet was a white woolly head.

'Chill out,' said Elliot. 'I know what I'm going to do.'

'What?' I asked, leaning over to stroke Snowy's head. 'They'll totally hash you . . . and then they'll know you're not really Elliot McCoy. Rigg might even be there. he'll arrest us on the spot!'

'I told you, it's sorted,' said Elliot, putting down his sandwich and jumping out of bed. 'I'm a man with a plan. And now, if you'll get out, I'd like to get dressed.'

I had to leave it at that. I decided that Elliot should pretend to be ill. But when I got downstairs, Elliot's hoverboard had gone from the hall. The front door was open and Liz was just leaving for work, wearing the silky grey dress with the raindrop sequins.

'See you later, petal,' she said, pointing to a note stuck to the front door. 'Elliot left this for you.'

Deer H
I had to get in erly becos of the chess thing
See you later
Chill out
Its cule
E

I was distracted by a delicious smell coming from the kitchen. Sky was in there standing over a frying pan, with Snowy sitting at her feet, gazing up at her longingly. The smell of the cooking hit me in a wave of homesickness.

'Look at this,' I said, showing her Elliot's note. 'He says he's got it sorted, but I'm worried.'

Sky scanned the note, smiling as she flipped the bacon. 'If he's not worrying about it, why should we? Maybe he's going to go sick or something.'

'Maybe . . . but what are you doing? What's wrong with the reppy?'

'Nothing's wrong with the reppy. I asked Liz if she could find some real bacon. She warned me that raw meat was a very dangerous ingredient. I said I'd take the risk; I like cooking. Would you like some?'

I looked at the sizzling frying pan.

'You bet.'

We perched on the high kitchen stools to eat. We didn't

have any real bread, so I got some toast and ketchup from the reppy and we made bacon sandwiches.

'It's nice, isn't it?' she said.

I nodded. I had a lump in my throat.

'Won't be long now,' said Sky.

'I know,' I said, and we set off for school together on our hoverboards. I hoped that Sky would get another invitation to the Palace soon. Then we could get it all over and done with.

The chess tournament went on all day. The final was to be held after school at four o'clock, in the music room. There was a prize of four thousand pounds for the winner. The finalist's names were to be posted up in the entrance foyer at three-thirty. I headed down there with Sky and we watched as Miss Trump spoke softly into her projector. 3D words appeared in the air.

Congratulations to our Chess Finalists!
Rachel Marx (Westminster)
Elliot McCoy (Regents House)

There weren't that many people up in the music room. Mr Slater was there and some kids from Elliot's class and a few people from the other school. Stella Rigg was there too, and Marc Marquez. The spectators' seats were arranged in a circle. In the centre were two chairs and a table with a chess set.

I was looking at the chess pieces when I felt a touch on my shoulder. It was Elliot, looking a bit strained.

'Well done, mate,' I said. 'And good luck.'

'Thanks . . . but I think I've done well enough already.

I'm not going to try and win this one,' he whispered. 'It wouldn't be fair.'

I didn't have time to reply, because who should walk in next but Miss Trump with President Rigg himself. I felt quite sick when I saw him and the effect on the rest of the room was electric. Everyone shot to their feet and smartened themselves up. Miss Trump looked more terrified than anyone, and she sat down at the back as soon as she'd shown him in.

'Relax,' shouted Rigg. 'Sit down everybody. Pretend I'm not here.'

'Sit next to me, Daddy,' said Stella.

Rigg made his way over to her, but on the way he clapped his hand on Elliot's shoulder.

'Well done, old son,' he said. 'I like a boy who knows how to fight for his school. Win this, and you and the other two can come round for a special victory supper on Friday. What do you say?'

Elliot looked startled.

'What's wrong, son? Scared of the androids?' said Rigg, putting his huge hands round Elliot's thin neck and pretending to strangle him. 'There's nothing to fear, boy, we'll scan you in first this time, don't worry!'

Elliot looked at Sky and me for guidance. We both nodded furiously.

'Thank you, Mr President,' said Elliot, rubbing his sore neck. 'We'd love to come.'

'It's a deal,' said Rigg and he clapped Elliot hard on the back again and went to join Stella and poor old Marc Marquez.

'Elliot has to win now,' whispered Sky. 'Do you think he can?'

I shrugged my shoulders and watched as Elliot's opponent arrived. As she sat down, she shook Elliot's hand in a really friendly way and gave him a big smile. Elliot smiled too, but when it faded he looked terribly shifty.

I don't know much about chess, but I tried to follow the game, which was projected simultaneously in 3D. They both started out by moving their pawns and hopping the knights about a bit. Rachel Marx was smiling and alert. She was enjoying herself. Elliot looked nervous. Rachel took one of Elliot's knights then one of his bishops. Even I could tell that Elliot was in trouble. Then Elliot put his head in his hands and stared at his opponent. It was as if he was thinking carefully what his next move should be. I saw Rachel's head slump ever so slightly. Elliot made a move and Rachel responded by taking his remaining knight. There was a gasp from some of the more knowledgeable members of the audience. Rachel had obviously made an elementary mistake and Elliot took her queen. The game went on. Rachel made several more terrible blunders and it was soon checkmate. It was an easy victory for Elliot.

I couldn't tell whether Miss Trump looked disappointed or relieved as she congratulated Elliot. As for Rachel Marx, she looked confused.

'I don't know what happened to me,' she said to Elliot as she turned to go. 'I'm sorry I didn't give you a better game.'

'I know what happened, young lady,' said Rigg heartily.

'You were thrashed by a superior opponent. Well done, young Elliot.'

'Thanks,' said Elliot weakly, as Rigg thumped him on the back yet again.

'I'll see you and your brother and sister at the Palace on Friday,' he boomed. 'Come on Stella.'

I went over to congratulate Elliot myself. How on earth could he have made the hypnosis work in such a nerve-racking situation?

'That was brilliant, Elliot,' I said.

'Hardly brilliant,' said Mr Slater. 'The president is entitled to his opinion, of course, and I'm sure we're all glad that Elliot won, but I thought the standard of play this year was absolutely appalling. I'm going to write to the Board of Education!'

'I still say it was brilliant,' I whispered to Elliot. 'How could you do the hypnosis with Rigg in the room?'

'I've been asking Mr Slater for extra help in the Relaxation classes,' he said glumly.

'And you've got us all invited to the Palace on Friday,' said Sky softly as we made our way down the stairs. 'Nice work, Elliot.'

But Elliot said nothing at all until we got home.

'Cheer up, Elliot,' I said, handing him a bottle of CloudNine. 'You did really well.'

'I didn't.'

'You did.'

'I didn't. I cheated all day long. That prize meant a lot to Rachel Marx. She told me at lunchtime, if she won she was going to use it to go and see her dad in Canada. She hasn't seen him for four years.'

My mum or dad would have known what to say, but I didn't.

'I wish we'd never been fast forwarded here,' said Elliot.

'Well, it won't be long now,' said Sky. 'Do you want something to eat, Elliot?'

'No thanks,' he said. 'That reppy food sucks,' and he called Snowy and went off early to bed.

It was a quiet evening. Liz and Sky looked through the movie archives for an old film we all liked. They chose *The Man in the Iron Mask* with that actor from *Titanic*.

'Are you and Elliot taught to fight with swords like that?' said Liz seriously.

'No,' I said. 'That was a bit before our time.'

I'd seen the film before, years ago, and I still enjoyed it. But, like the bacon, it made me feel homesick.

14
Elliot Strikes Back

I was late leaving school on Thursday, because I had to help AJ Sherif with our group's presentation on robotics. When I got home, there was a note stuck to the hall mirror.

> Deer H
> I know what to do about the chess munny
> I have gone swiming with Sky
> Meet us down at the pool if your hard enuf
> ps rigs sekritry rang to comferm supper at the palace
> tomorrow RISULT!

So we *were* going back to the Palace tomorrow. I felt sick. I went up to my bathroom, got changed and launched myself off into the flume. I recognised the music from school assembly. It was the *William Tell* overture and it cheered me up. As I flew along headfirst in the jet of warm water, I realised that if it went well at the Palace, we would all be home by Friday night. I just had to stay cool and keep Elliot safe until then.

Down in the pool, Elliot was back in his usual good mood. He had a soaking wet Snowy with him and he and

Sky were throwing a ball to him. Pets weren't allowed in there, but as it was our last ever swim, he didn't care if he got caught. He explained what he was going to do about the money. He was going to ask Stan to give it to Rachel after we'd gone home, with a letter explaining that he'd cheated.

Back on the nineteenth floor, Liz had arranged the games room table for a formal conference. There was a plate of cookies, and glasses and place names in front of the ten chairs, which read: Doll, Elliot, Finn, Hunter, Lewis, Liz, Sky, Stan, Steiner and Wilson.

Lewis, Finn and Doll were the first to arrive.

'Our heroes,' said Finn, holding out his arms to us, while Doll handed us an enormous bunch of flowers. 'We'll give you a real thank you present later.'

Then they made some weird clicking noises to each other and disappeared into Liz's study. I looked at Lewis in alarm.

'It's their private language,' he said. 'Take no notice, Hunter, they've just gone to make a few last improvements to their virus.'

Steiner arrived next and then Stan.

'I am honoured to make your acquaintance, Stanley,' said Steiner. 'We are so grateful to you for liberating Doll. I always knew a clone could be a great asset to the operation.'

Stan shook Steiner's hand, and then turned to me.

'Yo, timelord,' he said. 'How's it going?'

'Not too bad,' I said. 'How are you?'

'I'm cool,' said Stan. 'I've got rid of my lodgers. Doll

wiped their memories and we parted the best of friends. Brilliant person that Doll.'

'Do you think her and Finn's virus will work against the androids?' said Sky.

'It better,' said Elliot. 'He's going to send them out on the streets soon.'

'No he isn't,' said Stan. 'Because we're going to stop him, aren't we Hunter?'

'You bet,' I said, trying to sound confident.

'Nothing can stop us now,' said Stan. 'I've got some great news about Ed, Stella's driver . . .'

'Is that the one who landed them on the balcony?' said Lewis.

'That's the one,' said Stan. 'Rigg got him to do hundreds of press-ups as a punishment, in front of everybody. Ed is furious. So I went to see him and suggested we taught Rigg a lesson, by giving him a security scare. Ed was up for it. He's going to give you a lift up to the balcony room at eight pm and his mate's going to make sure all the cameras close down at the same time. So there'll be nothing showing on Rigg's screens when you need to upload the virus.'

Then Wilson arrived and Steiner called us all to the table. Finn and Doll came back in and exchanged enthusiastic hugs with Stan. Steiner asked Wilson to pour water for everybody and Liz handed round the cookies. Then Steiner stood up and addressed us all.

'Tonight is a historic eve,' he said. 'As you know, Elliot has obtained a second invitation to the Palace tomorrow, thanks to his brilliance at the chess tournament.'

'It wasn't brilliance,' said Elliot. 'Just the old hypnosis.'

'Now, now Elliot,' said Steiner. 'Even Doll admits that brainfeed never worked. You did very well and we're all very proud of you.'

'Whatever,' said Elliot, and Steiner continued.

'On the first visit – which Sky was efficient enough to arrange in her very first week here – Hunter cleverly managed to locate the system access point in the main balcony room. Finn has since completed the virus that will disable the whole system. With Doll's enhancements, it will even shut down the androids. As soon as Hunter uploads the virus tomorrow, all the cameras, alarms and automatic weapons will shut down, including the new android guards.

'Then we strike,' said Steiner, crashing his fist theatrically on the table. 'However, there is still the risk of attack while Hunter, Sky and Elliot make their way to the balcony room,' he continued, blowing on his smarting fingers. 'We must ensure that the security screens are blank then and that the androids do not attack.'

'You can leave the security screens to me and Stella's driver, Ed,' said Stan. 'We've got it covered.'

'Terrific,' said Steiner, selecting a nice big cookie and biting into it.

'And you can leave the android guards to me,' said Wilson. 'My Palace contacts are poised. They will make sure that the faces of Sky, Elliot and Hunter are scanned into the permanent Palace staff file. They will be perfectly safe from attack.'

Wilson looked unusually buoyant. He had his feet on a chair and he was chewing gum.

'Are you sure you know what you're doing, Wilson?' said Lewis.

'Yes,' said Sky. 'You didn't even know about the androids a week ago.'

'I know exactly what I'm doing, young lady,' he said and he gave her a beaming smile.

'Now is everything clear?' said Steiner. 'Sky, Elliot and Hunter will appear to leave the Palace at eight pm, but Ed will, in fact, land them back on the balcony. Sky and Elliot will stand lookout at the two entrances to the balcony room, while Hunter loads up the virus.'

I suddenly had a brainwave.

'Hang on,' I said. 'Now Stan's with us, he can upload the virus, can't he?'

'That's right,' said Lewis. 'He's a clone, so he can go anywhere in the Palace. There's no need to put Sky and the boys in danger.'

'Sorry guys,' said Stan. 'Clones are like Daleks; we can't go upstairs. Rigg really doesn't trust us, you see. We're confined to the ground floor and he's even got sensors on the lifts and stairs. And although you can make minor mods to Palace admin from the downstairs control room, you can only get at the core security system from Rigg's private access points on the top floors.'

'You three are still our only hope,' said Liz, apologetically. 'Have a cookie.'

'Do you have the virus here to show us?' Steiner asked Finn.

'It's in Liz's computer,' said Finn.

'Go and get it, will you Wilson?' said Steiner.

Wilson gave Steiner a funny look, took his feet off the chair and went off to Liz's study. He came back with a wafer-thin gold card.

Steiner took it from him with a nod.

'A tiny thing,' he said. 'But its powers are mighty and its consequences huge. With the androids out and the security system down, Rigg will be pretty well defenceless. Our sources think very few clones will stay loyal to him. He'll either run or we'll arrest him. I hope to be able to get him for crimes against humanity.'

In a dramatic gesture he held the card aloft.

'This virus means freedom for Finn and Doll; an end to bullying and terror; and a return to peace and justice.'

'And home,' I said to Elliot.

After the meeting, Wilson had to go and arrange for our faces to be scanned into the Palace staff file. Liz asked everyone else to stay for a final supper. She was in a party mood and she went to set it up on the big table in the games room.

Liz didn't want any help so I joined Doll and Finn who were resting on the sofa. They were snoring gently, but they both had one beady black eye open.

'Poor things,' said Lewis. 'They've been working night and day on that virus.'

But they leapt up when Liz stuck her head round the door and announced that the feast was ready.

'I thought you were asleep?' I said to Doll.

'We were and we weren't,' said Doll. 'Finn and I only

ever shut down one half of our brains at a time. It's a genetic thing.'

'That's how dolphins sleep without drowning,' said Finn.

I never thought Liz took a blind bit of notice of what we ate, but the feast she'd laid out included all our favourite things. There were plates of sausages in buns, bacon rolls, burgers and lightning chips. There was a curry, a bowl of steaming rice, spaghetti and meatballs, salads and a big bowl of squid stew. There was also a plate of flaming crepes suzettes, a huge baked Alaska, a stack of Sparx bars, a large glass jug of CloudNine and a bottle of red wine.

Liz started handing round plates.

'Eat, drink and be merry!' she said. 'For tomorrow we die.'

Elliot looked horrified and put his plate down.

'It's just an expression, Elliot,' said Sky reassuringly. 'Get stuck in.'

We went round heaping our plates with food then sat down around the big table.

'To Operation Timewarp!' said Steiner, holding his glass high.

'Nothing can stop us now!' said Liz, raising her wine glass with him.

But the glass fell from her hand, and a pool of blood-red wine spread out over the table, as the balcony doors burst open and two armed clones crashed into the room.

One of them grabbed Steiner and held a gun to his head and the other did the same with Liz. I raised my stun gun but dropped it at once when the first clone shouted:

'Drop your weapons or the old guy gets it!'

'That's more like it,' said the other one, who had a vicious expression and a completely shaven head. 'Tie 'em up, Rio,' he said to his mate, who was wearing fancy cowboy boots.

They were the clones from the old warehouse.

Snowy certainly recognised Rio; he was snarling and snapping at his cowboy boots.

'Not you again,' said Rio. 'Get off, you stupid little dog.'

He kicked out hard at Snowy, who yelped and slunk off to hide under the snooker table. Then Rio flung a reel of tape over to the bald-headed guard, who pushed Steiner back into his chair and strapped him to it. He did the same with all the rest of us. Then a third man stepped through the balcony doors.

His face was shadowed by a hood, but his stout figure and soft voice were instantly recognisable:

'Well, that was nice and easy wasn't it?' he said. 'You disappoint me, Steiner. I thought your team might have been capable of a bit more resistance.'

'Wilson?' said Steiner. 'Tell this goon to release me. What the hell are you doing?'

'I'll tell you exactly what I'm doing,' said Wilson. 'I'm putting a stop to your pathetic plan to overthrow the President.'

He poured himself a glass of wine.

'I haven't told Rigg yet,' he continued, sitting down and putting his feet up on the table. 'But I'm really looking forward to it.'

'I don't believe it,' said Steiner.

'Let me explain,' said Wilson. 'When you first conceived this ridiculous operation, I knew it would get us all into very serious trouble. But you just don't listen to advice, do you? I had no choice but to sabotage it. First I nobbled the ladder. Then I introduced a bug into the swimming brainfeed. There were several more disappointing failures. I began to think it was true what they say on those ads, maybe that cloudy drink the kids are into really does give you nine lives. Then I suddenly realised it was for the best. I would let you go nearly all the way. Then I could foil your plot at the eleventh hour and gain Rigg's eternal gratitude.

'I was through with you and this was a chance to get back in with Rigg,' he said, draining his glass and refilling it. 'I bided my time. I kept a track on the kids using that silly little dog so I knew what they were up to with Doll. I decided to let them get on with it. I knew Rigg would be furious about Doll's escape and I thought he would be most impressed if I could hand Doll back to him as well as giving him Finn's time machine. And he'll be ever so grateful that I've uncovered your nasty plot. Now that Finn and Doll have completed the virus, I have all the evidence I need. He'll make me London Mayor at least, don't you think?'

'But Wilson,' said Steiner, 'you were my right-hand man. I trusted you implicitly.'

'More fool you,' cackled Wilson. 'I sometimes give you full-fat yak's milk cappuccinos, you know, and get them lightly dusted with dried camel dung. And you never even notice! Little things like that have kept me going through all the years you've bossed me around. You and your slices of flipping lemon. You and your show of respect for Finn and Doll and the young people. All you've ever been interested in is your own power and glory. Well, it's my turn now and I'm making the most of it. I can't wait to see Rigg's look of gratitude when I turn you in.'

'What about us?' said Elliot.

'That's up to President Rigg,' said Wilson. 'But I hardly think he'll offer you a lift back home.'

While Wilson was talking, I was trying desperately to relax enough to use the Jedi thing, but after two or three failed attempts, I had to give up in despair.

I tried to catch Elliot's eye, but the guard with the shaved head was now giving me a very nasty look. I tried to mime a Jedi knight using his light sabre, but it was difficult with my arms bound to my sides. I added sound effects:

'Phoioing . . . phoioing . . . phoioing.'

The clone glared at me.

'Shut up!' he snarled.

But Elliot took several long deep breaths and stared hard at Wilson.

Slowly, Wilson walked over to the large games cupboard and crawled in under the bottom shelf. The two clones looked at each other, mystified. Then Elliot focused on the bald one and he put down his gun, and followed Wilson into the cupboard.

'Are you crazy?' yelled Rio. Then a dreamy look came over him too and he put down his gun and followed the other two, shutting the door behind him.

Snowy came out from behind the sofa and bounded over to Elliot, wagging his tail. Elliot struggled out of his bindings, leapt to his feet and pushed the wall button that locked the cupboard shut.

'How skilled was that?' he said with a huge grin on his face.

'Astonishing,' said Steiner, as we all freed ourselves. 'How on earth did you do it, Elliot?'

'He used his hypnosis, of course,' said Lewis.

'Based on my work,' said Doll proudly.

'Wild,' said Stan.

'What did you tell them to do, Elliot?' said Sky.

'I told them to put down their weapons, walk into the cupboard, shut the door behind them and sit quietly thinking about shades of blue, like we do in relaxation classes.'

'I was going to make them jump off the balcony,' I said.

'Like people wouldn't notice if a load of clones fell on their heads,' said Elliot.

'You did very well, Elliot,' said Steiner. 'You saved us all. If I hadn't seen the hypnosis with my own eyes, I would never have believed it possible. I owe you an apology, Hunter, for not believing you when you first told me about it.'

'That's all right,' I said.

'They must be well crammed up in there,' said Lewis.

'They seem happy enough,' said Sky. 'Listen.'

'Navy blue, sky blue, sea blue.'

'Mm, lovely, I can almost hear the waves.'

'Turquoise.'

'Nice one.'

'Ultramarine.'

'Far out.'

'Danish blue.'

'That's not a colour, it's a cheese.'

'OK then, emerald blue.'

'Emeralds are not blue.'

'What are they then?'

'They're green, you idiot.'

'No they're not. If they're not blue, I reckon they're red.'

'They are not.'

'They are.'

A scuffle broke out inside the cupboard.

'The hypnosis wears off without eye contact,' I whispered. 'What shall we do?'

'Stun them, I think,' said Steiner quietly. 'Would you three do the honours?'

'I'll get Rio,' said Elliot.

'I'll get Wilson,' I said.

'I'll get the slaphead,' said Sky.

'And I'll get the door,' said Lewis.

We took our stun guns and crept into position. Lewis pressed the button to unlock the cupboard door and it swung slowly open. The three men were still crouching down under the bottom shelf. They saw us and made to spring up, but we opened fire immediately and three limp bodies sprawled on the carpet.

'Three out of three,' said Stan. 'Not bad.'

Steiner slumped back into his chair.

'Full-fat yak's milk,' he said to himself. 'Who would have believed Wilson would turn out to be such a traitor?'

And why had I wasted so much time worrying about Miss Trump?

Elliot was struggling to pull one of the highly polished cowboy boots off Rio's lifeless foot.

'My name is Elliot McCoylius,' he said. 'Owner of an injured dog. And I will have my vengeance in this life or the next.'

The boot came off in a rush and Elliot fell over backwards.

'Come on, Snowy,' he said, picking himself up and holding the boot out to him. 'Tasty leather,' he coaxed. 'Chew it up . . . that's a good boy!'

Snowy carried the boot off to his beanbag for a good chomp. I turned round to show Sky, but she was staring out of the window looking worried.

'What about scanning our faces into the Palace employee file?' she said. 'Who's going to do that now we can't trust Wilson?'

'Stan?' said Lewis.

'Could you tell me how, Finn?'

'Of course I could, man,' said Finn. 'It'll be easy for you. you can borrow Ed's ID card and walk right into the Palace. No problem.'

We said a rather solemn goodbye, and then Finn, Doll and Lewis took the three unconscious bodies off to a safe place. Stan went to scan our faces into the Palace staff file and Steiner and Liz went out to make last minute arrangements. We decided to have an early night, but the doorbell rang. I went to answer it.

It was Miss Trump. She was even more nervous than usual.

'Call the others please, Hunter,' she said. 'I want to speak to you all.'

Sky and Elliot came down, followed by an excited Snowy, who bounded down the stairs and skidded to a halt on the polished floor. Miss Trump remained hovering in the doorway.

'I won't come in,' she said, giving Snowy's head a timid pat. 'I just wanted to give you my blessing. I'm aware I haven't been as welcoming to you as I might have been. To be honest, I was never in favour of Steiner's plan. I felt that your presence put the whole school at risk. Nor did I approve of sending three young people on such a dangerous operation. However, you have been very courageous so far and I just hope you come out of it all unscathed. Good luck.'

She shook our hands and scuttled off to the lift, leaving us feeling jumpy.

'Never mind her,' said Elliot, as we went upstairs. 'Only one more boss to go, then we've completed the whole thing.'

'What are you on about?' said Sky.

'It's like a game, isn't it,' said Elliot. 'With levels and bosses. We've had the green-eyed dog, the clones at the pool, Doll's prison, the clones in the warehouse and Wilson's coup. Now it's Rigg and his androids. He's the worst boss, but it's the last level. Then we've completed it all and we can go back home.'

'Are you homesick?' said Sky.

Elliot nodded.

'So am I,' I said.

'Me too,' said Sky. 'But I'm going to miss Liz and the apartment and the pool.'

'And the hoverboards,' said Elliot. 'And Snowy.'

'And Stan,' I said.

'And Stella,' said Elliot grinning. 'You'll miss her the most, won't you Hunter?'

I closed my bedroom door on him. In bed I thought about what Elliot had said about Rigg. I hoped he wouldn't be as hard to defeat as your average PlayStation boss. They're all right once you've worked them out, but you never beat them the first time.

I woke in the middle of the night. There was no point trying to go to sleep again, so I went down to get myself something from the reppy. Sky was already down there, watching a film with the volume turned right down.

'I can't sleep either,' she said, switching the 3D image off.

'Have some hot chocolate with me then.'

'OK.'

I asked for two hot chocolates. Then I asked for two blueberry bagels, as an afterthought, and the reppy gave us two fresh apricots on the side.

Sky munched hers thoughtfully.

'Do you think we'll be all right at the Palace?' she asked, looking straight at me with her big brown eyes.

'I don't know,' I said truthfully. 'It's Elliot I'm worried about.'

'Elliot?'

'When we arrived, Finn warned me that Elliot was in danger.'

'You're joking.'

'No. From someone with owl eyes.'

'Must have been Wilson.'

The round tinted glasses. Why hadn't I thought of that?

'Or an android,' I said. 'But if he did mean Wilson, the danger's over.'

'Have you told Elliot?'

I shook my head.

'You didn't even think of telling me?'

'After he'd warned me, Finn took it back. Then I decided he was nuts. Then I sort of forgot about it until we met those androids. Then I thought Elliot could avoid going back to the Palace, but this chess thing means he has to; he's the guest of honour.'

'Don't worry,' she said. 'I'll help you look after him. We won't let anything bad happen to Elliot.'

'Do you think we'll see each other much when we get back?' I said.

'We're bound to, aren't we?'

'Good,' I said, finishing off my bagel.

'And don't forget Lewis . . . I'll have to get used to living with him again.'

'Maybe that won't be so bad, now you know him better,' I said.

'Maybe,' she said, brushing the bagel crumbs off her silver pyjamas. 'We might learn to get along.'

'You can always come over to ours,' I said. 'If you get fed up.'

She nodded. We sat there for a while looking out of the big windows and finishing the hot chocolate. After a while the sun came out over the rooftops. It was time to wake Elliot up for school.

part three
Results

15
Showdown at
the Palace

'Hello Ed,' said Stella to her driver. 'You remember the
McCoys, don't you? Sky, Hunter and Elliot.'

'Course I do,' said Ed in his nice friendly voice. 'Hop in.
Do you three fancy landing on the balcony again?'

'No way,' said Elliot, pulling down his collar to show the
bruising on his neck. 'We've only just recovered from last
time.'

Ed winced when he saw the bruise and shook his head.

'I do not approve of these androids,' he said. 'Your old
man's gone too far this time, Stella.'

Stella looked annoyed. She ignored Ed and started
talking to Sky about her new shoes.

'See you later McCoys,' said Ed, as he landed us down at
the main entrance. 'I'll meet you back down here at eight
o'clock, sharp. We don't want you in the Palace any later
than that, do we?' and he gave us a conspiratorial wink.
'Make sure you get them scanned in properly this time,
Stella.'

'I was going to,' said Stella sniffily. 'You don't have to
keep going on about it.'

Another clone met us in the magnificent entrance hall and led us to the control room. There were androids guarding the lift and the foot of the stairs. Elliot walked very close beside me. The androids' heads were turning constantly, and they all seemed to spot us at the same time. Their bodies tensed as if to sprint towards us.

'Cease,' shouted the clone, and the androids relaxed and turned away.

'Here we are, safe and sound,' said Stella, showing us into the control room.

There were two clones and several more androids in there. The androids turned, as one man, to stare at us.

'Cease,' shouted Elliot.

The androids flexed to spring.

'Cease,' shouted one of the clones, who wore a badge labelled Tel. 'It's no good you talking to them, boy,' he said to Elliot. 'They only respond to Rigg and us clones.'

The androids went back to scanning the huge bank of screens, which covered a whole wall of the room. Their heads tilted up and down and rotated from side to side, covering every nook and cranny of the Palace.

'What do they do if they spot somebody they don't recognise on one of those screens?' said Sky.

'They hunt 'em down,' said Tel with a sinister laugh. 'And they attack . . . you do not want to know how.'

'Yeah,' said the other clone. 'The Palace has been on red alert since that freaky Doll escaped. So Rigg's got the androids set to kill now.'

'How do they kill?' said Elliot, trying to sound casual. 'Do they strangle you?'

'That's one of their methods,' said Tel, nodding grimly. 'But they've got others. Shall we get 'em to show their teeth?' he asked his colleague.

'You shouldn't really, it's classified, isn't it . . . all the androids' attack methods is classified information.'

'Go on . . . they're only kids . . . they're not the enemy.'

Tel turned to the nearest android.

'Open wide,' he said.

The android's hinged jaws opened impossibly wide, revealing glass teeth like two rows of short, sharp icicles.

We all flinched and took a step back. The two clones chuckled.

'Now, what've we got that we don't need?' said Tel, looking around. 'That old brolly will do, we don't know whose it is.'

He picked up an umbrella that was standing in the corner of the room. He approached the open-mouthed android, jabbing the sharp end of the umbrella at its face.

'Attack,' he said.

The android's jaws snapped shut around the umbrella with a clang. It ground its teeth from side to side for a moment, and then opened up again, so that the splintered pieces of umbrella fell with a clatter onto the cold stone floor. Some bits of black material were still stuck in the sharp points of its teeth.

Elliot clutched my arm so tightly that it hurt.

The clones laughed gleefully.

'You should have seen 'em catching those squirrels in the

grounds,' said Tel. 'And that stray dog that came in, did you hear about that, Stella?'

'That's horrible,' Sky said angrily. 'It's not funny at all, it's disgusting . . .'

I shook Sky's arm to get her to stop and she fell silent. But the damage had been done.

Tel looked at Sky with surprise, and then raised his eyebrows at Stella.

'Bit of a loudmouth isn't she? Are you sure your dad approves of your new friends?'

'Of course he does,' said Stella, impatiently. 'He's the one who invited them. Now scan them in until eight pm please, and get on with it, we don't want to stay down here all evening.'

As before, Tel told us to stand in front of the large screen on the wall and we saw a clear picture of our faces in it, like a reflection.

'Request security clearance,' he said. 'Start time – now. End time – eight pm,' he said. 'There you are, sorted, no nasty toothmarks on you when you go home tonight.'

'That's that done,' said Stella and she swept out of the room, without even bothering to say thank you or good-bye.

'Stuck-up, that sister of ours, isn't she?' I heard Tel whisper to his colleague, and then I started to follow Stella and the others out of the room.

'Goodbye, kids,' said Tel. 'Have fun.'

As I paused in the doorway to say goodbye, Tel turned to his mate:

'Oy! Come and look at this,' he said. 'There's an alert

from the system. It's saying those three faces are already . . .'

Then the heavy metal door swung shut behind me, cutting off the sound of his voice.

I didn't have time to worry about it though, because I had to run after Stella and the others, who were just getting into the lift. I didn't want to get left on my own in that entrance hall with all those clones and androids.

Stella was dead keen to do some more recording up in her studio. For an hour or so, we forgot everything and got into it. Stella wanted to do a version of this song 'Lost in the Stars'. So she and Sky hummed it in and I created a video background of a starship with long white corridors and huge windows looking out onto the infinity of space. Stella and Sky danced along the corridors and Elliot and I sat on the bridge, looking out at the stars, playing keyboards and drums.

'Let's put an alien in,' said Stella.

So Elliot made one a bit like the three-eyed aliens in the vending machine in Toy Story. He put a lot of effort into his design and then he copied it to make a whole chorus line of them. Stella loved them.

'They're brilliant, Elliot,' she said. 'Look at them singing outside the window.'

I didn't really need to make an effort with Stella any more, but like last time, I fiddled around to make her seem more special. I added this echo to her voice and extra shine to her eyes. She was dead pleased with it all.

'This is fantastic fun,' she said. 'I'm so glad you came to my school, Sky. You and your brothers.'

Just before seven, we set off down to the next floor, to meet Rigg for supper. There were two androids standing at the bottom of the grand staircase. I froze when they looked up, but they took no notice of us. Their heads went on tilting and rotating, sweeping the stairs with their enormous staring eyes. Our faces were obviously safely scanned in, but it wasn't easy walking past their powerful, swaying bodies, tensed to sprint and attack.

'I wish I hadn't seen their teeth,' said Elliot.

'We're eating in here,' said Stella, pushing open the heavy glass door into the dining room. 'I hope Dad's ready 'cos I'm starving.'

'So am I,' said Elliot, cheering up.

The dining room was absolutely massive. There were tapestries on the walls and huge glass chandeliers hanging from the ceiling. Two long tables ran the whole length of the room, flanked by enough golden chairs to seat an army. I wondered if all the clones sat down to feast here every day. As we walked down the middle of the two long tables I spotted Rigg. He was sitting on a red and gold throne on a kind of stage at the far end of the room. It made even his bulky body look small.

'Welcome,' he boomed. 'Got past the boys in one piece then, eh?'

We did our best to join in his laughter. Then he told us to sit down. I'd been wondering if the androids might provide a terrifying waiter service, but Rigg drew back a heavy red curtain to reveal an ordinary food replicator.

'What can I get you?' he asked. 'Ladies first I think,' he said, leering at Sky.

'I'd like a tuna salad please, with a glass of mineral water,' she said.

'Is that all?' said Rigg. 'Not on a diet are you, with your lovely figure? Let me get you a little treat to go with it, something chocolaty maybe. What do you say?'

'Thank you,' said Sky, politely. 'That would be very nice.'

Rigg asked the reppy for Sky's salad and a chocolate and cherry mousse to go with it. I noticed you didn't have to say please to his machine. The mousse came in a tall glass with a long, thin spoon.

Stella chose to have the same as Sky. I didn't think I'd be able to eat at all, so I just asked for cheese on toast, but Elliot asked for sausage and chips and beans and pizza. Rigg himself had liver and bacon. He ordered us all one of those tall chocolate mousses for pudding.

I couldn't eat much and Sky just pushed her food around, but Elliot tucked in hungrily. His extra Relaxation lessons were really paying off.

'This is a really nice tea,' he said to Rigg.

'Good. I like a boy with a healthy appetite. You're a plucky little lad, aren't you? You eat well, you speak up nicely and you're good at chess.'

'Not that good,' said Elliot.

'And you're modest with it. You remind me of myself when I was a boy.'

Elliot choked on a bit of pizza, and had to have several sips of water before he could continue stuffing down his chips.

'What do you like doing, when you're not at school?' Rigg asked.

'I quite like Ju-Jitsu,' said Elliot, without thinking.

'Ju-Whatsu?' said Rigg in a puzzled voice. 'Ju-Jitsu? Isn't that some sort of martial art? I didn't know kids these days went in for that sort of thing.'

'No, no,' I interrupted, a bit too quickly. 'Ju-Jitsu is just . . . the name of our dog. Elliot means he likes playing with our dog, training him . . .'

'I thought your dog was called Snowy?' said Stella.

'That's just what I call him,' said Sky.

'That's right,' I said. 'Me and Elliot call him Ju-Jitsu . . . because . . . because he wrestles with us on the floor, not that we know anything about martial arts, but we saw an old film with it in . . . just by accident . . . it happened to be on . . . and sometimes we call him Jitsy for short . . .'

Sky kicked me hard under the table and I shut up.

Rigg was looking at me strangely.

'Let's all have pudding,' he said, reaching for his mousse.

'You know what they say, Hunter,' he said softly, passing me one of the long silver spoons. 'He who sups with the devil must use a very long spoon.'

I didn't know what to say to that, so I just ate my mousse. It was probably very nice, but I was too nervous to taste it. I was just glad when Rigg looked at his watch and announced that it was nearly eight o'clock. He pushed back his chair.

'Goodbye,' he said. 'I've enjoyed finding out a bit more about you . . . what do you call yourselves?'

'The McCoys,' said Stella.

'Ah, yes . . . the McCoys,' he said. 'Of course. I looked

you up on my system the last time you came. You've only recently moved to London, haven't you, and you're living with your aunt, while your mother has some surgery?'

We nodded nervously.

'You must be missing your mother, Sky,' he said.

'Yes, I am,' said Sky, truthfully.

'And you hope to be back with her again soon?'

'Yes,' said Sky, looking rather alarmed. 'I hope so, if everything goes well.'

'I'm sure you're all looking forward to that, aren't you?' he said, looking round at us.

We nodded.

'Well, what will be will be,' said Rigg, standing up and wiping his mouth with a golden napkin. 'Though in my experience, things don't always go according to plan.' And he crumpled up the napkin in one fist, tossed it on the floor and marched out of the room.

Elliot went to pick it up.

'Leave it, Elliot,' said Stella. 'The maids will clear up.'

'We'd better get going,' I said.

'What a shame,' said Stella. 'Still, you can come again next week. You will, won't you?'

'We'll come if we can,' said Sky.

'You bet,' said Elliot, under his breath. 'Unless we happen to be sucked back into the past by a loony old man with a time machine.'

The next part all went smoothly. We said goodbye to Stella just before eight, and her clone driver, Ed, flew us up above the Palace rooftop.

'Do you think Rigg is onto us?' I said.

'Maybe,' said Sky.

'I don't,' said Elliot. 'Anyway, it doesn't matter now, does it, because we've nearly completed the whole thing.'

Ed was nervous and didn't say a word until he'd taken us down to the balcony again.

'Take care,' he said, as we jumped softly down onto the balcony. 'Stan says to tell you that he's downstairs – and the screens are all off.' Then he gave us a thumbs-up sign and flew off.

It was good to know that Stan was in the building. It gave us the courage to creep into the big green and gold room. We hid for a moment behind the heavy curtains. There didn't seem to be anybody around, so I headed for the Pinocchio desk and Sky and Elliot went to stand guard at the doors.

I touched the little statue and the desk opened up, revealing a screen and a small card slot. The little card containing Finn's virus was in the leg pocket of my cargo trousers. I was reaching down to get it when I heard the unmistakable sound of powerful android footsteps. I fought the urge to run. The android would take no notice of me, because my face was scanned into the employee file. I tried to look relaxed as the android's menacing face appeared in a distant doorway. It stared at me for an instant. Then to my horror, it pounded straight towards me.

'Run!' yelled Sky.

All three of us pelted off into the next room, with Elliot in the lead. I saw Sky dart to the left and hide behind a heavy golden curtain. I did the same and it was a terrible mistake. It left Elliot to run on into the next room – alone. I heard the android pound past us in pursuit of Elliot. Then there was silence.

This was it. Finn's premonition. The owl eyes and Elliot in danger. The dreadful realisation paralysed me. Fortunately, Sky took charge.

'Stan must have made a mistake scanning in our faces,' she whispered, tugging at my sleeve. 'Give me Finn's card. I'll go back and upload the virus. You go and help Elliot. Try the hypnosis.'

I gave her the card and she darted off, without a backward glance.

The hypnosis wouldn't work, but I knew I had to do something. I crept over to the thick blue curtain that draped one side of the doorway to the next room. The room was a dead end; there were no further doors on the other side. There was no sign of Elliot either. The only thing moving in there was the android. I held my breath and watched as it worked its way methodically round the room. Each time it came to a window, it snatched up the heavy curtains that draped it. Each time it did so my heart missed a beat, but Elliot wasn't behind any of them. When it came to the last set of windows it opened them carefully and looked out. Perhaps it hoped to find Elliot sitting on the window ledge. The breeze from the open window set all the blue curtains waving and flapping. Out of the corner of my eye I saw something else flutter in the wind. It was a flap of silver material sticking out of the door of a cupboard. It was the same colour as Elliot's shirt!

The cupboard had ornate golden touches, so maybe the

android wouldn't notice the tiny scrap of silver? It closed the windows and continued round the room examining every piece of furniture. It opened a black cupboard with two little Chinese vases on top. They were those dragon vases with tiny golden bells on and I heard them jingle.

Then the android opened a small carved box on a table. Did it really think Elliot could be in there? Then it opened a writing desk. It even opened the tiny hidden drawers, designed to hold pens and letters. So much for artificial intelligence. I noticed that it closed everything up again carefully, almost tenderly. However rough the androids were with living things, they'd obviously been programmed to take care of Rigg's valuable possessions.

It was Elliot's cupboard next. I knew I had to do something and I felt strangely calm. I took out my stun gun silently, then slammed it against the wall to release the trigger handle. The android glanced round briefly at the noise, then crouched down and touched the scrap of silver material. I took aim and fired. Bam! The android sprang round. It pulled out the dart, looked at it and put it carefully in its pocket. Then it scanned the whole room with its huge staring eyes. I shrank back again behind the curtain. I don't think it saw me, but it lifted its head and gave a shrill whistle – the call for backup.

Then it turned back to Elliot's cupboard again. Without stopping to think, I ran into the room and grabbed one of the Chinese vases. Then, using a move I'd learnt in the basketball brainfeed, I jumped up high behind the android, and slammed the vase down on its head. It shattered into a million pieces, and the android whirled round and punched me hard in the stomach. I'd never felt anything like that punch. It left me fighting for breath among the sharp shards of china, while the android turned back to the cupboard.

Before it could open it, I staggered to my feet and grabbed one end of the long blue rug it was standing on. I gave a sharp tug, using my whole body weight to pull the rug from under its feet. We both fell over, but the android was up first. It hauled me upright, then knocked all the wind out of me with another sledgehammer punch.

Then it turned back to the cupboard, wrenched the door open, dragged Elliot out, grabbed his collar and held him high up with his feet dangling in the air.

I'd never seen Elliot look so terrified, but he tried to smile at me.

'Beam me up, Scotty,' he said.

I ran and jumped on the android's back, trying to cling onto its thick neck.

'Hang on!' said Elliot as the android tried to shake me off.

Then we heard another pair of pounding feet approaching and we knew it was all over.

The first android tore me off its back and flung me hard into a corner of the room. Then it grabbed Elliot's arms, held them behind his back and forced his head down. The second android came up close, opened its hinged jaws wide and bent over Elliot's head. It was going to bite Elliot's whole head off, like one of those snakes that can swallow a whole chicken. Its glass teeth were glinting and Elliot's face was twisted with pain. I stumbled towards them while

Elliot struggled desperately to escape, when, suddenly, both androids froze rigid.

Elliot wriggled free of the one that had been gripping him. Then, with one finger, he gently pushed the one whose jaws were opened in attack. It toppled over, with a heavy thump and a tinny clatter from its internal workings. Rigor mortis.

Elliot put a foot on top of its head.

'I am invincible,' he said shakily and then sat down on the floor.

'That was very close,' I said, sitting down next to him. 'It took ages for Sky to upload the virus.'

'But you held them off all right,' said Elliot, looking at the mess on the floor. 'Did you smash something when I was in the cupboard?'

'One of those little black vases with dragons and bells on.'

Elliot looked down at the broken pieces, picked up one of the tiny golden bells and put it in his pocket.

'Bet that was worth a fortune,' he said, looking round for another bell.

'Come on, Elliot, leave that stuff, let's go and find Sky.'

'Hang on a minute,' he said.

'COME ON, Elliot!' I shouted – and ran for the door.

'Coming,' he said, but he lingered for a moment and when I looked back he was looking shifty.

We ran back the way we'd come and met Sky running towards us.

'Are you all right?' she said to Elliot, breathlessly. 'It took me ages.'

'No worries,' said Elliot. 'Hunter held them off for just long enough.'

'Brilliant,' she said and she gave him a big hug.

'Hey,' she said. 'What have you got under your shirt?'

'Nothing,' said Elliot.

'Well done Sky,' I said. 'You saved our lives.'

'But it seemed to take for ever. I'd nearly finished uploading the virus when another flipping android ran past. I hid just in time but it stayed in the room for ages. When it finally left I came out and tried again. Then another one appeared, but it suddenly froze and fell over. The virus must have kicked in . . . the whole security system has shut down.'

'We've done it,' I said. 'We can go home!'

'But what do we do now?' said Elliot.

'We go back to the balcony,' said Sky. 'Steiner will be there . . . with Lewis . . . and the time machine.'

But when we got out on the balcony, there was nothing. There was the golden statue, lit up as usual, and the distant lights of hovercars – going about their business as if nothing dramatic was happening. Behind us in the Palace, it was a different story. We heard gunfire and the sound of an explosion. The stone beneath our feet shook. Sky gave me a worried look and Elliot clutched my arm.

Then we heard a welcome humming noise and saw a familiar, battered old shape approaching. It hovered above us and Steiner's face appeared, leaning out of the window. He looked old and tired, but very happy.

'Is everything all right?' said Sky. 'We can hear fighting.'

'It's under control,' said Steiner, lowering the metal

steps. 'But get in quickly now – it's not over yet – and it's time you went home. You've done your bit and done it with great courage, but I don't want to expose you to any further danger.'

We didn't argue. We climbed straight in and Steiner started off. Lewis was in there and he had a nasty cut above his eye. He shook my hand.

'Thank God you're all safe,' he said.

Just then a clone ran out onto the balcony. He was armed with a kind of missile launcher, which he pointed right at us.

'Land that hover, or I shoot,' he yelled.

Steiner did as the clone said. He had no choice.

Then, as the guard started to open the hatch, Lewis did an amazing thing.

'I'll jump him and keep him out of action for as long as I can,' he whispered to Steiner. 'You fly the others out.'

Steiner nodded.

'No, Lewis,' said Sky, and she grabbed his shirt to hold onto him. Elliot grabbed it too, but Lewis shook them off. As the hatch opened, he jumped on the clone and knocked him over. They struggled together on the ground and Steiner started to take us up.

'Stop Steiner!' I shouted. 'You can't leave Lewis there. That guard will kill him.'

'You're right,' muttered Steiner and he started to take us down again.

Then another clone ran out. It was Stan and I've never been more pleased to see anyone in my life. He pulled the clone off Lewis and spoke to him urgently. Then he waved to Steiner, who took us right down and opened the glass bubble. Stan scrambled in with Lewis. He looked elated.

'A misunderstanding,' he said. 'Sorry about that. You're a brave man, Lewis.'

Lewis glowed.

Stan looked at us.

'Good job, McCoys,' he said, excitedly. 'You've shut Rigg down.'

'It was nothing,' said Sky modestly.

'I nearly got my head bitten off,' said Elliot. 'I don't call that nothing.'

Stan grinned.

'You were great,' he said. 'All of you.'

'I'm taking them out now, Stan,' said Steiner.

'It's goodbye then, timelords,' said Stan, giving us each a hug.

'Goodbye, Stan,' said Elliot. 'You're a clone in a million.'

'Yes,' I said. 'We were lucky to bump into you.'

'I was the lucky one, Hunter, to see you jump off that diving board to save your brother. You were scared; you could hardly swim; but you still did it. It gave me the courage to make my own leap, and I'll never forget it.

'Take care of them, Steiner,' he said and he vaulted out.

Then we soared up through the night sky. Looking back through blurred eyes I could see that parts of the Palace were burning and there were groups of men fighting in the grounds.

'There's a lot of fighting going on,' I said to Steiner. 'What about that sanctity of human life thing?'

'You've got too used to our reppy food, Hunter,' he said, dryly. 'You've forgotten that you can't make an omelette without breaking eggs.'

16
Home

Steiner drove without lights. We had several near collisions as we headed south out of London, but we survived. We had lots of questions for him.

'Why did the androids attack us?' I said.

Steiner was squinting intently at the traffic and he didn't seem to hear.

'I said why did the androids attack us, Steiner?'

'Yes . . . sorry about that . . . rather unfortunate . . . a guard on duty in the control room noticed you'd been scanned into the permanent staff file. He thought it was a mistake and he deleted you.'

'Didn't you and Finn realise that might happen?' I said.

Steiner ignored me and winced as we narrowly missed another hover. He was a pretty terrible driver.

'Can Finn and Doll come out of hiding now?' said Sky.

'Not yet I think.'

'What have you done with Rigg?' said Elliot.

'We haven't found him yet,' said Steiner, with a touch of irritation. 'What do you expect? The system has only been down for a few minutes.'

'Of course,' I said soothingly. 'It's early days.'

He can be a touchy old gentleman, that Steiner.

'These things take time you know,' he said. 'Rigg may be holed up somewhere, but his androids are down, his security system is dead and most of the clones are with Stan. Those androids turned the clones against Rigg, so his days of glory are numbered.'

'Good,' said Sky. Then she turned to Lewis and touched his cut head.

'That's nasty,' she said.

'You should see the other bloke,' said Lewis.

'Did you get in another fight before then?' said Elliot, admiringly.

'Yeah,' said Lewis. 'I had to fight my way past a couple of clones just to get into the hover.'

Steiner raised his bushy eyebrows.

'Cool,' said Elliot.

'Not,' said Lewis. 'I slipped running up some steps and cut my eye on a bollard.'

Sky laughed and punched Lewis on the shoulder.

'You were very brave to tackle that clone on the balcony,' she said. 'You saved our lives.'

Lewis shrugged. He really was a pretty cool guy.

'Me and Hunter fought the androids,' said Elliot proudly. 'And we won.'

'With a little help from Sky,' I said.

'I saved your bacon,' she said.

'But you took your time about it,' said Elliot.

'Tell us everything that happened,' said Sky. 'When I was uploading the virus.'

I told them how Elliot hid in the cupboard and how I attacked the android with the stun gun and the vase. Then I described how it was going to bite Elliot with its sharp glass teeth.

'Not glass,' said Steiner. 'Diamond, apparently.'

'Rats,' said Elliot. 'We could have snapped some off and taken them home.'

Steiner looked rather shocked.

'At least I got this,' said Elliot, pulling up his shirt.

It was the little Chinese vase with golden dragons and bells on, the twin to the one I broke.

Steiner started in his seat and we almost smashed into a tall tree. It must have been Finn's old tree, because he took us down to land with a bump.

'You shouldn't have taken that vase, Elliot,' said Steiner.

Elliot looked stubborn.

'You shouldn't have exposed us to those androids,' he said. 'This vase is our fee, our danger money. I thought we could sell it and share the proceeds four ways.'

Which just shows, you can live with someone all your life, and they still do things you're not expecting.

We all looked at Steiner to see what he would say.

'The matching one's smashed,' I said. 'They'll think this one was too.'

'Anyway,' said Elliot. 'I had to spend all my skateboard money on those manky old contact lenses and nobody ever paid me back.'

'Put the vase away, Elliot,' said Steiner. 'You can do what you like with it. I never saw it and I know nothing about it.'

'You'll be glad one day,' said Elliot. 'I'm not nicking it,

I'm preserving it. I've thought it all out. We take this one back to the past, which means that there's three. Then when Hunter smashes the other one in the future, there'll still be a matching pair, won't there?'

Steiner ignored him. He was busy setting the time switch. He sent out the probe and I leaned over and looked at the little screen. I could see the hover outlined against the empty garage.

'It's time for us to say goodbye,' said Steiner, who looked quite solemn. 'I don't know how to thank you all. You achieved all I could have hoped for . . . and more. You helped us overthrow Rigg. You prevented the deployment of those terrible androids . . . and you even found Doll,' he said, giving Lewis a special look. 'You have also been great company. It's been good to see real, flawed young people in action.'

'Flawed?' said Elliot, hugging his vase. 'Us?'

'We've enjoyed it too,' said Sky. 'Haven't we, boys?'

'Not half,' said Lewis. 'It was hectic.'

'You probably won't want to tell anyone about all this,' said Steiner.

'Too right,' I said. 'They'd think we were insane.'

'But perhaps you'll be able to use your influence one day. Remind people that it takes all sorts to make a world. Then Rigg may never happen.'

What influence would we ever have? I thought, but I nodded seriously.

'By the way,' said Steiner to me. 'Doll says you and Elliot shouldn't use your powers of hypnosis again. She never meant it to be used on people against their will.'

'OK,' said Elliot, but I noticed his fingers were crossed.

I didn't have to say anything, because we were interrupted by a sudden sharp tap. It was Liz, rapping on the glass bubble with her ringed fingers. Finn was standing next to her waving delightedly.

'Open up,' they shouted and Steiner put the glass bubble right up.

Liz leant in, her usually sleek hair a tangled mop.

'Have you been in a fight too?' said Sky.

'We came down on a hoverbike,' said Liz, smoothing down her hair. 'We just had to come and congratulate you all. I am so proud of you.'

'We-hey!' said Finn. 'You were fantastic.'

'They've got Rigg, by the way,' Liz said to Steiner.

'Excellent. Excellent. Where was he?'

'He took off with Stella, but the driver, Ed, turned them in. Rigg is in a cell and Stan took Stella to Miss Trump's. She can stay with her until her mother comes to get her.'

'Poor old Stella,' said Sky.

'I brought you these, my dears,' said Liz, passing me a bag and a large box. The bag contained the clothes we were wearing on the day we left. The box contained a warm ball of fluffy white fur.

Elliot's face lit up.

'He's sedated,' said Liz. 'But he'll wake up in an hour or so. I thought he would miss you all . . . especially you, Elliot.'

Elliot turned to me.

'Do you think Mum will let us keep him?' he said, running his fingers through Snowy's warm fur.

'I don't know,' I said. 'We could say we found him abandoned in our shed . . . she just might.'

'Thanks Liz,' said Elliot.

'Thank you,' said Liz, leaning over to kiss each of us goodbye. 'You've been . . . inspirational.'

'This is for you, too,' said Finn, handing Lewis an enormous parcel tied with a big red ribbon. 'A big thank you from Doll and me. Open it when you get home.'

We thanked them both and said goodbye again. Steiner hauled himself out and handed me a slip of paper and the three of them stepped back.

'It's all set to take you back to the time you left. Just press *Go* when you're ready,' shouted Steiner. 'When you get there, send it straight back to us. I've written the date and time on that paper, Hunter. Set the machine to *Go* and get out as quick as you can. Goodbye now. Take care.'

Sky leant over and pressed *Go*. Then we were off. My head felt like it was going to explode again . . . and we were there. The other three got out with the stuff and I reset the machine. I pressed *Go*, then leapt out just in time to see the hover disappear.

Tara looked at the bag of clothes.

'That's that then,' she said. 'We'd better get changed.'

She changed in the garage and the rest of us changed at the base of the ladder. We looked like something out of an old film.

'Wonder what's in Finn's parcel?' said Elliot.

'Let's open it up in the shed,' said Lewis.

'What shall we do with all this stuff?' I said, holding up

my metallic clothes, the leather boots and the stun gun in
its holster.

'Hide it,' said Elliot.

'Are you really going to sell that vase?' said Tara.

'You bet,' said Elliot. 'I may have to sell it on the black
market. I'm not going to do anything hasty.'

I looked at Elliot with astonishment. What did he know
about the black market?

'My dad might be able to help,' said Lewis.

'OK,' said Elliot.

Lewis took Snowy and went up the ladder first, Elliot
took the vase and went up after him. Tara watched him
climb.

'At least we kept him safe,' she said. 'From the owl eyes
and all that.'

'We did,' I said. 'But he shouldn't have been exposed to
all that danger in the first place, should he?'

'That's what Miss Trump thought, I suppose,' said
Tara. 'Steiner didn't care. He just wanted Rigg out.'

We followed the others up and I had no fear of the high
ladder at all.

In the shed, we tore the wrapping paper off Finn's
parcel. Four brand new hoverboards fell out. They were all
the same: dark red on the underside, with a small golden
wasp and the FlyBoy logo at one end.

'Wow!' said Lewis. 'I saw these on display in Harrods.
They're the top of the FlyBoy range.'

'Cool,' said Elliot, picking one up and hugging it to his
chest. 'But when can we ever use them?'

'At night,' said Sky, her eyes gleaming.

'I just hope Finn hasn't tried to customise them,' I said, thinking about the erratic performance of my stun gun and his kettle.

We pushed open the splintered shed door and picked our way through the brambles to the barbed wire fence. The roll of bin bags was still there. I picked it up and we stuffed the hoverboards, the vase, the clothes and Snowy's box inside the black bags. Lewis crawled out under the fence and we passed the bags over to him. We shared out the load and walked up to our back garden wall.

'See you later then,' I said to Tara and Lewis.

'OK,' said Tara.

'We could call round when Snowy wakes up?' said Elliot. 'We need to buy him some food. We could all take him down to the shops for a walk.'

'Good plan,' said Lewis. 'But you don't need to go to the shops yet. I've got loads of dog food.'

We looked puzzled.

'I keep it for feeding hedgehogs,' he said.

Which just shows, you can live near someone all your life and not know the first thing about them.

So that really was that. We went back to an empty house, we destroyed the note we had written before we left and we hid our special clothes, the hoverboards and the vase in the drawers under Elliot's bed. Then we took Snowy for a walk with Tara and Lewis. After that we waited for Mum to come home from work. It was great to see her, and the funny thing was that she seemed really pleased to see us, even though she didn't even know we'd been away.

She made us scrambled eggs on toast and Elliot cried. He had to say he burnt his tongue and then he started laughing and couldn't stop for about ten minutes.

Life soon went back to normal. We would have liked to know what happened to Stan and Liz and Finn and Doll and Steiner and Stella – even Rigg and Wilson. Sadly, there was no way we could find out.

It took a while to persuade Mum to keep Snowy, but now she loves him. Once he got this nasty swelling by his ear. The vet removed a tiny gadget that was implanted in there – he'd never seen anything like it – and he gave it to us to keep.

'Must be a tracking device,' said Lewis as we all walked home. 'So Wilson and his men could follow you around.'

'That's why they were waiting for us after we got Doll out,' said Tara.

When term started, they noticed our swimming, of course. I'll never forget the look on Mr Venning's face when I dived in and cruised past the whole class. He went quite pale and had to sit down on the tiled floor.

Dad couldn't believe it either. Mum rang him up and told him to take us to Tooting Bec Lido, which is a massive open-air pool near his flat in London. It's freezing there, but we showed him what we could do. He's proud of us, but he's puzzled and I'd like to tell him the truth.

Tara keeps up the swimming. She trains every day and she's in the county team. I'm not so keen, but I swim for the school and it's great to be good at a sport.

During a wet playtime, Elliot's teacher at primary school noticed his chess skills. She got him to enter a competition and he won. She asked him where he'd learnt to play chess like that and do you know what he went and said?

'It came to me in a dream.'

'You wally,' I said, when he told me about it. 'Why didn't you say you taught yourself from a book or a CD-ROM or something?'

'I didn't think of it,' said Elliot. 'She put me on the spot.'

So now they think he's some kind of mystic.

'It's funny how a stupid thing like that can change how people treat you,' said Elliot. 'I'm still the same person, but now I get a bit of respect.'

'Not from me,' I said, but I didn't mean it. I have a weird kind of respect for most people I meet these days. Like Steiner said, it takes all sorts to make a world . . . well, nearly all sorts anyway.

The chess thing puzzled our mum though. Elliot wanted to tell her the truth and it was awkward. Another thing that puzzled everyone was the ladder and tunnel from the shed to the garage. The police even came to look at it. They thought it might have been used by drug dealers and they sealed it off.

Sometimes we met at night and flew our hoverboards. We were very careful not to be seen, but somebody must have spotted us, because a blurry photo of all four of us flying over the golf course appeared in the papers, under the heading *Aliens or Hoaxers?* As Lewis said, those golfers really put the hours in.

As for the hypnosis, we agreed to use it only for emergencies. I had to use it on Lewis's old mate Daniel and his gang. I had no choice, because they kept jumping Lewis and me on the way back from school. I got them to skip about holding hands in a ring and I only had to do it once.

We did sell Elliot's vase. Tara suggested that we bought a big box of old junk at the car boot sale and pretended to find the vase in amongst it. It was a good plan and it worked.

The vase turned out to be from the year 1790 and it was painted with real platinum and gold. The experts said it matched a pair of vases in Buckingham Palace, but we already knew that, didn't we? They also found some fibres of silver material snagged on the dragons. The fibres were found to have an unknown molecular structure – and they remain a mystery. You would not believe how much it was worth – enough for a whole fleet of skateboards. Elliot split the money four ways with Tara, Lewis and me and the money changed our lives quite a bit.

Not that those changes were anything compared to the upheavals when Stan got back in touch – but that is another story.